Finn Carling

Commission

*Translated from the Norwegian
and with a Foreword by*
Louis A. Muinzer

Peter Owen
London & Chester Springs PA

U.S. DISTRIBUTOR
DUFOUR EDITIONS
CHESTER SPRINGS,
PA 19425-0007
(610) 458-5005

For Liv

PETER OWEN PUBLISHERS
73 Kenway Road London SW5 0RE
Peter Owen books are distributed in the USA by
Dufour Editions Inc. Chester Springs PA 19425–0449

Originally published as *Oppdrag*
First published in Great Britain 1993
© Finn Carling 1991
English language translation © Louis A. Muinzer 1993

ISBN 0–7206–0896–1

A catalogue record for this book is available
from the British Library

Printed and made in Great Britain

Foreword

Like *Under the Evening Sky*, the first novel by Finn Carling to be
translated into English, *Commission* (*Oppdrag*, 1991) displays the
Norwegian author's two major hallmarks as a writer: a rigorous
economy of expression that pares a narrative to its essentials and
structures it with the skill of a watchmaker, and a brave devotion to
worthy human themes – loneliness, social injustice, family relationships and the nature of both art and the artist. On a more homely
level, it also displays his fondness for international settings and
characters, as well as that most Carlingesque of traits: the use of
animals to advance a theme and enhance a story.

But *Commission* is anything but 'typical Carling': it is a very
curious *tour de force* – the work of a mature artist/craftsman who has
set himself an almost impossible task and achieved it against the
odds. For considered in conventional terms, this award-winning
novel should be something of a bore. It has a lacklustre title and tired
chapter headings like 'Dialogue about a Piece of Jewellery' and
'Monologue about an Experiment'. It features a narrator who is so
isolated and repressed that his style is impersonal to the point of
exasperation. True enough, the story he is drawn into by a wealthy
and eccentric family resembles a traditional thriller, for it explores
the mysterious death of young Sebastian Warden. At the end of the
hunt, however, the reader isn't quite sure what happened, let alone
who did it. And no wonder, for the facts of 'the Sebastian case' are
confused by the contradictory accounts of the characters and up-
staged by the wanderings of a nameless dog.

And yet the reader who ventures into the mind, style and world of

Finn Carling's drab story-teller has an unforgettable adventure in store for him. That adventure hinges upon an irony: the man behind the novel's impersonal, seemingly bloodless voice is a famous author, presumably English, whose life and words have dried up. He has abandoned not only his family and his career but his human unique-ness – his 'I'-ness – and has become an impersonal 'one'. *Commission* does not so much concern his reluctant pursuit of his writing assign-ment as the return of his own personality through contact with the curious people of Carling's novel – above all, with the dead Sebastian himself and the remarkable dog.

For *Commission* is a thriller of a very special kind: a thriller that sets its scene in the mean streets of an isolated personality. As in the case of all thrillers, its ending must be experienced, not disclosed. Suffice to say that it is deeply satisfying, highly affirmative and dis-tinctly grammatical – an exciting read that *one* will long remember.

In the original the narrator of *Commission*, who is always 'one' and never 'I', challenges Carling's Norwegian readers. He and his story also challenge an English translator – to say the least! In undertaking the task, I am grateful to have had the encouragement and inspired editorial assistance of Michael Levien, with whom I worked on *Under the Evening Sky*. Without his friendly guidance, the following text would have been much the poorer. I am grateful, too, to Finn Carling himself, who very kindly read a late draft of the translation and gave it his approval. Once again, in accordance with the author's usual practice, reported speech is printed without quotation marks.

Louis A. Muinzer

Contents

The Harbour

The rooms are as barren as cells. That doesn't matter, for the windows have no bars, the door is unlocked. One's stay isn't forced on one by others, but by an inner necessity.

As a kind of last way out.

The house lies at the top of a street of steps. If one lifts one's eyes one looks out over the garden wall, olive trees and moss-grown roofs towards the harbour. The fishing-boats have arrived with the morning's catch of squid, and black-clad women have been at the pier and made their purchases.

As they do every day.

The world is no larger. The daily repetition is a blessing, the moment overshadowing all. Leaves room for neither past nor future, neither memory nor dream. Thought is concerned only with when one shall get up and if the weather is good enough for one to stroll down to the pavement café at the harbour for a small glass of pastis and water before walking home for a rest.

It almost always is.

A word processor is standing on a worn-down old oak table. A necessity, one thought. But on an island like Corsica the current can suddenly go off, and the text on the screen disappear before one's eyes. As if it had never been written.

That means nothing any more, either.

But one thought stands there as long as the current lasts:

In the beginning was not the word, but the experience. Words that don't disappear and leave the experience standing there naked are like conceited messengers who believe themselves more important than what they have come to deliver. Like dancers so thrilled by their own elegance that their movements are veiled and incapable of moving. Or like writers who are so preoccupied with being writers that they search desperately for words instead of opening themselves to experience.

At the pavement café in the village harbour, all movements are slow. It takes an eternity to raise a glass of pastis to one's lips, sip from it and put it down again. The fishermen, the black-clad women and children are only parts of a tableau, like the boats and the houses. Every time one looks up, the tableau has altered. The fishermen, the women and the children are standing differently, as if someone has moved them slightly.

Sometimes a newspaper is left on the table. Usually in a language one doesn't know. That doesn't matter, for the letters make an attractive pattern against the marble top. It is difficult to remember when one looked at a newspaper in any other way.

Outside every café there is music coming from loudspeakers. It always sounds the same. On rare occasions it stops, and there is a voice speaking in a foreign language. French? Italian? On arrival, one made out individual words: Lebanon, Thatcher, Kabul. It was like listening to a conversation one has nothing to do with. But now the words aren't words any longer, just variants of the music.

The street of steps from the harbour up to the house is a long one in the heat. For that reason, one goes walking late in the day, when the houses have begun to cast shadows.

The dog is sitting at the gateway. It is always being chased away, but it comes back. Its thin body merges into the garden wall. One doesn't see it until it gets up. At first, it jumped away when one approached, but it was sitting there again next day.

One evening, it glided in like a shadow when the gate was opened and sat down at the door. It didn't slip into the house. Not then. Without thinking about it, one threw left-overs to it. It lay down and ate, as if it couldn't stand up like other dogs. It didn't wolf down its food either, but chewed each bite. Afterwards it rose slowly, walked over to a tree and lay down to sleep beneath it.

The next morning it was gone.

When the gate is opened, the dog goes in. But it pays no heed when one closes the gate and walks towards the house. It keeps its distance – will be neither patted nor talked to. It is impossible to know what it wants. Perhaps it just wants to exist.

The door is opened, and the dog lies down by the fireplace with half-closed eyes. Sometimes it looks at one. A strange expression, carefully appraising, but distant. It is impossible to imagine what is going on behind those brown eyes. Whether it cares for one or whether one is only something that makes gates and doors open and close.

From a letter that should have been posted long ago, but which has remained lying on the oak table:

When you were informed about this journey, you assumed that it would give one the opportunity to work undisturbed. One has got that. But it has no purpose. Only ten years ago, we still believed we had a responsibility, could change the world. Or perhaps it was something we imagined. Do you remember how often you said in despair: Why struggle for years over a poetry collection that hardly a hundred people will read? That will just be carrion for critics?

Now one has no faith any longer.

There is nothing left to write about, either.

Of late, one has been like a thief in memory's secret garden. A person who cuts flowers from old plants and groups them into ingenious bouquets. Gradually, the plants began to wither between one's fingers. 'Memory's secret garden' became hardly secret and grew exhausted as well. Each detail of one's life had been ransacked.

At last, there was nothing more to extract.

Besides, there is something one has never said, not even to those nearest to one: Nothing concerns one any more. The expectation that one should rejoice in one's son's success, be charmed by one's grandchildren and lament the decline and death of one's friends became unbearable. One merely disappeared into oneself when one's grandchildren crawled on to one's lap, or an old friend yet again mentioned his cataract or possible stomach cancer, and thought: When can one get away from here?

One day is like another. Now and then it rains, some mornings are cool. It is of no consequence. In any case, one gets up and has breakfast. A cup of coffee and a croissant. If the weather permits, one walks down to the harbour, in order – after a glass of pastis – to walk back up to the house again, rest and eat a late dinner.

Time doesn't just stand still: it is abolished. The outside world doesn't intrude. The telephone left on the wall in the kitchen has never rung. One hasn't even checked to see if it works. From time to time a letter is written. But they aren't sent, so none arrives either. There is neither radio, television nor any newspaper in the house, just a few old books that can be read over and over when one can't sleep.

As when one is a child – or old.

Dialogue about a Piece of Jewellery

One morning something unpleasant occurs. A letter is thrust in beneath the door-knocker.

The letter is restrained, but behind the cool words one senses a desperation that is not expressed. The letter writer is a woman. The handwriting gives the impression that she is of one's own age. After apologizing for the letter, she writes that she would very much like to visit one the next day. She is travelling to Paris, but can take a plane via Corsica, where one lives. If it isn't inconvenient.

It is all very polite, to be sure, but she gives one no opportunity to beg off. Neither telephone number nor address – just the signature, Penelope Warden, and an indistinct postmark. It is taken for granted that one agrees.

This business of welcoming readers, which seemed gratifying in its time, seems questionable as time goes on. They often have expectations that exceed one's powers. Besides, what they have on their minds can be an excuse for getting close to an author they think they know through his books. So the day is spent tracking down the sender.

That one manages to reach her by telephone seems to be a matter of course . . . to Penelope Warden. Her voice is relaxed, and her choice of words strengthens the impression that she must be approaching fifty. One says that one can see her, but must learn what she wants.

She hesitates a moment, but answers calmly that her errand will hardly cause inconvenience, and that she therefore won't go into detail on the telephone. With equal politeness, one repeats that she will not be received if she doesn't disclose the purpose of her visit.

She possibly hesitates again, but her voice is as relaxed as before, as she says that she wishes to have a book written about a man who has taken his own life. The amount of the writing fee won't cause any problems.

One's immediate thought is to refuse her. But the unease behind her words makes it impossible to say no and be done with it. Of course it is made clear that one can hardly take on such a commission, but she can come nevertheless.

Well then, you'll see me at eleven!

If her voice hadn't been the same as on the telephone, one would hardly have realized that the woman coming through the door is the one who wrote the letter. Dark complexion and long black hair. A slender figure in white accentuates a youthful appearance. She is scarcely more than twenty.

I hope you haven't been waiting for me, she says, but I hired a car at the airport. It's pleasant, but when one doesn't know one's way about, it can be difficult to estimate the time.

Not only the voice but the choice of words is the same as on the telephone. It is incomprehensible. She must have noticed an uneasiness, for after sitting down she smiles cautiously and asks: Have I come at an awkward time, after all?

One shakes one's head.

But I can easily come back another day. I enjoy travelling, so it doesn't matter if I make a trip next week, for instance.

She means it. She takes aeroplanes as naturally as others take trams. One looks at her to find out what kind of a woman one has in one's house. She is used to that. Those dark eyes are calm as one lets one's glance glide boldly over her expressive immobility.

The collar on her white pullover slips down and reveals a necklace. Broad and apparently heavy, it gives her figure an impression of floating lightness. It is gold with a patterned, curved surface. Seldom does one see anything so attractive. But it is shockingly dented, twisted and bent like the mudguard on a much-used bicycle.

One hears oneself say that either she must put the necklace away or allow one to repair it. That it is impossible to talk to her, if one has to look at such a mistreated piece of jewellery. How in heaven's name did it get like that?

She blushes almost imperceptibly.

I don't know, she says, and touches the necklace as if noticing for the first time that it is not as it always has been. Is it so bad? Perhaps it's because I wear it all the time and it gets squeezed up when I'm sleeping. It's stupid, but I've never thought about it.

Please hand it over!

She hands one the necklace across the table, like an obedient and trusting child. Doesn't imagine anything could happen to the piece.

The room with the tools in it is so small that she must stand while one tries to find out how one can avoid spoiling the necklace. One has never done such work before. It doesn't get any easier when she mentions that she has inherited the piece, which is worth a fortune.

There is no turning back. One has rashly given the impression one can manage it. Besides, it isn't necessary to talk when one is sitting bowed over some work. If one says something, it is as if one is thinking aloud to oneself.

Sebastian, the sounds run while one carefully taps on the dents, Sebastian was like a young god, and as a brother he was unique. So it's incomprehensible that he took his life.

Suddenly she laughs.

You should have seen him once at our country place in Provence. He sat completely naked in an old oak tree like a Pan and whispered seductively to me as I was having afternoon tea in the garden with Grandmother. She didn't understand a thing – just sat there chatting away about herself and her personal affairs – even when he climbed

down and made love to me against the knotty tree-trunk. It was as
much as we could do not to burst out laughing at the sight of
Grandmother, who just went on talking and talking while he stood
there naked, playfully caressing me.

Then she says wonderingly: His skin was soft and hairless like a
child's. Or a young girl's. You couldn't tell how old he was, and even
if we knew when he was born, we always thought of him as ageless.

She squats down, stretches out her hand and touches the hammer
which is laid aside while one is polishing. But she doesn't look at it.

If anyone deserves a book, it's Sebastian. A book about how
fantastic he was, and about what he meant to all who came to know
him. About everything he stood for. So you must write the book.
You'll get whatever you want, if only you'll do it!

Her fingers touch the necklace. Glide over it as if in loving memory.
At the same time, it is as if she isn't aware of what she is doing. Then
one asks if they have read any of the books one has written.

Why do you want to know that?

If you haven't read any, why do you want a stranger to write a book
about your brother?

She withdraws her hand.

When Sebastian was buried in Singapore, we spoke of having a
book written about him. Father thought that I should write it. Before
I started at the Sorbonne, I wrote poetry. But I'd never done anything like this. Then your name was mentioned – don't remember by
whom. But you'll hear that on the videos.

The videos?

Yes, the videos of the funeral.

For the first time during the repair work, one turns towards her.
She is expressionless, perhaps astonished that one is concerned about
why one was chosen and that one doesn't understand about the
videos. She bows her head and sighs. As if she thinks one is fussing
over trifles.

When we got together after the funeral, she explains absently,
someone or other – perhaps it was Bob, a friend of his who is always

full of amusing ideas – said that we ought to record it on video. Chiefly to preserve what we remembered of all those incredible notions of Sebastian's.

Do you mean to say that at the gathering after the funeral you set up video cameras and microphones?

Yes, of course. Why not?

She sits there at the oak table, looking at the necklace before she puts it on. It hasn't merely survived the repairs but has even become fit for wearing. She smiles cautiously at one: Next time I'll come to you!

Shouldn't you try to remember to take it off at night instead? Then you won't need to come here and have it repaired.

She shakes her head.

That won't work. I forget so easily.

Then she glances through the window. Perhaps the necklace doesn't matter to her – is just something she is used to wearing and never looks at.

Then she says: You'll write the book, won't you?

How shall one reply?

Then she picks up some photograph albums she must have placed on the floor when she came in. She begins to leaf through them slowly and say where the pictures were taken, and who he is with in them.

Though most are of Sebastian alone.

He is extraordinarily handsome. It is true he seems ageless. Could just as easily have been fifteen as thirty-five. But that is somehow without significance. Often he is naked, standing like Michelangelo's *David* or posing like an artist's model. His eyes betray a consciousness of being seen. How can one take such pictures of a brother and – as if it were the most natural thing in the world – show them to a stranger?

The slender form is a man's. But the long eyelashes and the smooth, hairless skin makes one think that it could have been a woman. Even the powerful face, which is frequently partly concealed by the half-length, blue-black hair, has something seductively girlish about it.

Didn't his beard grow at all?

Sebastian's beard? No, not at all. He had no hair under his arms or between his legs, either. At first we thought he was a late developer, then we were afraid there was something seriously wrong with him. But when he began to sleep with women, we realized that everything was all right. That it was just the way he was. A quite rare person.

There is something devotedly admiring and at the same time clinically cool about her voice. What creates this curious mixture of nearness and distance? She loved her brother. But as if she is presenting a case, she calls attention to the pictures of his naked body to be certain one sees that he didn't have a growth of hair like other men.

What kind of relationship did she have with him?

Penelope Warden took the plane on to Paris. Without a care. Does she understand the anxiety caused by one's undertaking such a commission? She knows that one may hesitate, but more or less deliberately assumes that one will fulfil her wishes.

It isn't arrogance but innocence. Maybe she thought one hesitates to negotiate and make conditions, the way conditions are negotiated and made in her world. She scarcely takes it seriously. Several times she assured one that money was no object. That there may be something else to negotiate, she probably doesn't imagine.

She took the albums with her. The video cassettes remain on the table. One didn't ask her to leave them: she merely assumed that one would like to look at them. That isn't so simple. If one looks at them, perhaps one will be bound to these people for ever.

Was *that* the reason for leaving them?

The cassettes remain lying on the table. One doesn't have a video recorder either. Besides, why must one be exposed to them? But down at the harbour there is a shop with video equipment. The next day, one reluctantly takes the cassettes there.

Strange. There is no sound. Was there ever any? And the pictures aren't clear. In any case, nothing indicates that it all takes place after a funeral. It is like a lavish birthday party. One sees that one person after another is telling stories which are constantly being interrupted by laughter and the drinking of toasts.

A couple of cassettes are sufficient. The stories, the laughter and the toasting are bewildering. Because there is no sound, merely the faces appear, and despair overshadows the merriment.

What kind of people are they?

Why will they erect a memorial to Sebastian? A book about how fantastic he was? His sister gave no impression that he deserved it. On the contrary, a veil of oblivion ought surely be cast over most of his doings.

Though why let it concern one?

But Sebastian doesn't let one go. After barely a week, a person knocks on the door. A woman tied to the dead man in a way that would never have occurred to one.

Dialogue about a Heart

Suddenly the dog raises its head. There must be an animal outside in the darkness. If there is someone coming, one usually hears the sound of his steps.

Then there was soft tapping with the knocker.

Uninvited guests are highly annoying, even if one is only dozing in front of the fire. One should never answer their knock. But the uninvited person may have heard something or seen one through the window. Therefore one gets up slowly and goes to the door.

A woman is standing outside. In the dim light it is difficult to see her, but she must be approaching forty and looks strikingly ordinary.

My name is Rose Mayfield, she says. If it isn't inconvenient, I'd very much like to talk about something that once meant life or death to me.

What should one say? One asks if she'd like to take her coat off. She shakes her head but loosens her belt as if to suggest that even if she doesn't wish to seem intrusive, she will settle down for a moment none the less.

It would have been most natural to show her into the study. One might have had a need for the distance a desk can give. But the thought of going back where one has tried in vain to work is not to be endured. Besides, the woman's life and death can't possibly concern one. The visit must be a misunderstanding, and it may be possible to get rid of her quickly.

21

Inviting her into the living-room may seem obliging. Therefore one suggests the kitchen. Could have suggested anything at all. She passes the living-room without a glance and walks to the kitchen table as if it were in a waiting-room.

After sitting down, she lets her coat slip from her shoulders, as she might have done at a table in a cafeteria. Then she lights a cigarette and, with an almost unconscious movement, draws the ashtray towards her.

As you know, she says, and looks down, I shouldn't smoke. But I can't always be thinking about the heart. Can I now?

There isn't much one can say to that, either.

Nevertheless one says: How do you mean – think about the heart?

She lifts her eyes and looks in front of her. She could just as well be frightened as surprised. It takes awhile before she says anything. As if she is appraising the situation and is in doubt whether to get up and leave or to remain seated.

Then she says: You are writing a book about Sebastian?

Has someone told you so?

She is expressionless, but seems relieved. Even if she didn't receive a reply, she has in any case the impression that one knows who Sebastian was. So she hasn't come to the wrong person.

But they've *asked* you to.

So she too assumes as a matter of course that the book will be written. But who is this woman who must have been close to Sebastian? One hasn't heard of her and can't possibly remember her from the videos made after the funeral. Besides, even if she had been there, one would hardly have noticed such an ordinary person.

She smiles.

I didn't know Sebastian then.

That was certainly a strange way to express oneself. What did she mean by it? She couldn't very well have made his acquaintance *after* he died!

She sits with the cigarette in her hand. The column of smoke rises and spreads itself beneath the lamp that hangs from the ceiling. She doesn't see it. Doesn't smoke either. Just stares in front of her, while the white ash grows longer and longer and threatens to fall on to the table beside the ashtray.

Then she says: Even if I never saw Sebastian, it's his fault I'm alive. Some years ago, the muscles in my heart began to waste. I didn't know that a young person could be affected by such a thing. The doctors merely answered my questions with fleeting smiles. Then I knew that I had a short time left, and actually I didn't exist any more. So the first time my heart stopped it didn't worry me. My husband Michael and the doctors thought either that I was too listless to grasp what had happened or that I didn't want to understand how serious it was. But I felt that I was already dead. That my heart stopped was only a corroborating ritual. Why did they struggle to get it beating again?

The doctors' evasive smiles and Michael's helpless encouragement seemed laughable. Whenever Michael held my hand or stroked my cheek, I thought: A man's sitting there holding a corpse by the hand and stroking its cheek! I knew he touched me, but wasn't there. Michael became a stranger. His despair and concern moved me, as one is moved by seeing the next of kin's struggle at a deathbed, but I was more absorbed by the fact that I must once have loved him. Sitting there at my bedside, he concerned me as little as the doctors who popped up, looked at me and vanished. Considerately, I let him stroke my cheek and hold my hand.

One hears what she is saying, but the cigarette is so short that one merely wonders if she will burn her fingers. She puts the butt in the ashtray in time, takes a fresh cigarette and lights it. After a few pulls, she sits there again with it in her hand.

One tries to catch her glance. But she looks straight through one. Perhaps she doesn't even do that. Perhaps she hasn't any glance to catch, because it is directed inwards.

Why in the world did she come?

Even the morning they said they'd got a new heart, I felt indifferent. I saw the doctors' cautious enthusiasm and Michael beaming in the belief that everything was all right. But I turned away. They whispered that I was too listless to understand, and I was relieved that I hadn't deprived them of their concern.

Suddenly it is as if she sees that there is another person sitting there, and one manages to nod as she continues: They spoke in low voices as they wheeled me into the operating-theatre. A doctor placed his hand reassuringly on my arm. It was laughable, for I had long since left my body and was like a consciousness out there in the room. From there, I saw the whole thing. How they divided my breastbone, bent it apart with a retractor and removed my diseased heart. I also heard what they said when they brought in the new one, cooled down and in a metal bowl. How handsome he was, they said. Why did *he* take his own life?

How does that concern one? one thinks.

When my body awakened after the operation, Michael and the doctors came into the sick-room proud and happy, as if after a successful birth. As if I had asked to be reborn! I knew that the one they took to be me was married to Michael. Nevertheless I thought: What is this intruder doing here? Perhaps in order not to wound him, I closed my eyes. I heard the doctors whisper: Be patient, Michael. She isn't conscious yet.

She smiles to herself and lights another cigarette, which she just sits holding in her hand, while the ash grows ever longer.

What a stranger a person can become, she says. If I hadn't known why he was there, I would hardly have recognized him. In wonder, I studied him feature by feature. An awkward man in his forties. Perhaps not ugly, but not good-looking either. A face without distinctive features. How could the person who had then been me live with this meaningless being? At last, I don't remember how many days later, I said: You must leave! I don't know you!

That ought to have pained me. I saw that he looked like an animal that stands face to face with an inescapable death and doesn't know what death is. Just feels a paralysing dread. But I repeated: You must leave! I don't know you!

One night the door was opened, she continued. A young woman was standing with her hand on the knob. She was Chinese. But so were most of the nurses. Besides, I couldn't tell one from the other. Even if I was surprised at being disturbed so late, I didn't wonder why she had come.

Then I saw that she wasn't wearing a uniform, but had on trousers and a shirt of the kind these people wear. Neither of us said anything. It struck me that I ought to ring for the night sister. But whatever the girl wanted of me, it was of no importance. After having looked at me for a while, she said almost without moving her lips: Rose Conway?

Which I was called when I was married to Michael. Not a muscle in my face moved. The girl came slowly over to the bed, took something from a shirt pocket and placed it on my pillow. Then she left the room and closed the door silently behind her.

In the light from the blue night-lamp above the door it looked like a piece of paper. Perhaps a message. But I was completely uninterested. Nevertheless I lit my reading lamp, picked up the paper and looked at it.

It wasn't a message, but a picture of a naked man on a beach. I can't explain it, but I knew he was the one I had got my heart from.

He was like a Greek statue. Never had I seen such a beautiful person. I couldn't put the picture away, but lay looking at it the whole night. At the same time, something happened to me. Slowly and for the first time since I'd learned of my diseased heart, my body was again filled by my consciousness. I felt it as if a power radiated from the naked figure in the picture over into my hands.

I understood that he was the only person I had ever loved. The night he died, we conceived each other. He gained a new life in me, and what had been me lived again through him.

Whether she has told this to others is not easy to say. But she must have said it to herself, over and over again. The words are so precise, the pauses so well placed. One doesn't look at her, just listens. When she has finished, one raises one's eyes. Her face is cool, quite different from her words. Has the experience become a story?

It feels necessary to say something: How did you find out who it was?

The cigarette-ash has grown so long that has fallen on to the table, and she is occupied with only that. She moistens her index finger and manages to lift the ash up into the ashtray.

Then she turns and looks at one.

I asked for the newspapers so that I could read about the transplant. It was one of the first in Singapore, so they suspected nothing. Killing was so common, on the other hand, that it was seldom mentioned. Nevertheless I found a short article about something the police thought was a murder. And a picture of the victim, Sebastian Warden. It was small and indistinct, but I recognized him at once from the picture the Chinese girl had placed on my pillow.

Have you any idea why she did that?

She shakes her head.

I found out that she was Sebastian's girl-friend and was called June something or other. Out there, Chinese people often have an English first name, you see. The Warden family looked after her, perhaps to give the relationship an appearance of respectability.

Suddenly she looks at one and says: That young girl couldn't have meant anything to him. Most of the men there have such girl-friends. More or less prostitutes of all kinds of breeds and blendings. An item of consumer goods.

She turns away. A thought or fantasy glides over her face, and the middle-aged woman looks like a girl in love.

But when she again looks at one, the young girl is gone, and she speaks so softly that one has to lean over the table to catch what she is saying.

When I heard you were writing about Sebastian, I thought *you* could say why she came that night. I shall never forget how she stood in the door and gazed at me. It was a matter of indifference to me then, for my self didn't exist. But since Sebastian became alive within me, she is always in my thoughts. I try to see what her eyes express. Hate? Or concern – which caused her to give me Sebastian? Would she have done it if she had loved him? Only you can answer me.

Rose, no book's being written about Sebastian, and no one has mentioned the Chinese girl before.

To bring her from the world where she finds herself, one speaks her name for the first time. But she continues undisturbed:

After we had conceived each other, I carried Sebastian as one does a child. I felt his movements inside me. Like a fish-tail in my stomach. Felt his heartbeat.

Michael and I never had a child.

At the time, I always felt a gnawing guilt. Our childlessness was my inadequacy. That dying heart was my inadequacy. Only when the Chinese girl gave me Sebastian did I understand that I was guiltless. How could I have a child with a stranger? What was more reasonable than my heart having to die?

Sebastian gave birth to my guiltlessness.

Remember that when you write about him!

Not even the dog notices her getting up. One sits there looking at her as she draws her coat up over her shoulders again and fastens her belt.

One hears her thank one for writing a book about Sebastian. It means so much that someone understands and puts words to what he was. No one else could have done it.

Afterwards, one tries reluctantly to remember her. To remember if one heard her close the front door. To remember if one caught a glimpse of her in the light from the street-lamp, when she should have gone through the gate.

Monologue about an Experiment

Journeys are intolerable. Railway stations, airports are flooded with people. Faces crowd in upon one with their indifference. With officious faith in their right to exist.

Out of the pushing and shoving there may emerge some who smile searchingly and mention something one has written, a spouse who has died, something they have or haven't done themselves. Or they come along with children they want one to smile at. Perhaps say something to.

Nevertheless one travels to meet Sebastian's older brother, Professor Wilhelm Warden. A voice on the telephone from Oxford late one evening: I believe you ought to visit me concerning Sebastian. It is unfortunately impossible for me to come to you. Of course we'll pay for your trip and your stay here. So I'll meet you at Heathrow tomorrow evening?

He asked. Out of politeness, not because he doubted that one was coming. One ought to have said no. When one is not going to write a book, there is no reason to expose oneself to a journey. And the very next day! In any case, nothing must be paid and commit one to carry out the commission.

Next evening one lands at Heathrow. Perhaps one recognizes him

29

from the videos made after Sebastian's funeral. Perhaps one realizes that it must be him, because of his attentively preoccupied manner. As if he looks for one, to be sure, but at the same time doesn't give his guest a thought.

He takes one's suitcase and says: My car's out here. After a long trip, it's pleasant to avoid the train. Besides, it's a pretty trip at this time of year, if it isn't too dark to see anything.

One is not driven to Warden's home but to a laboratory. Of course it is unimportant where the conversation takes place, if only it is over quickly. The professor must oversee an experiment. It concerns the response of nerve cells to stimulation in the form of flashing light.

Perhaps one would like to see?

Why not?

The experiment is being carried out in a dark-room, where there are fluorescent screens everywhere. It takes a moment before one sees the object of the research, a black cat with white paws and blaze on its forehead. It is almost lost in an apparatus that extends from floor to ceiling. Its paws are fastened with metal clamps, its head is held in place by a hoop with regulating screws, and some slender electrodes are inserted through holes in its cranium.

It lies staring motionlessly.

The professor explains: The cat is anaesthetized and will be put to death before it awakens. Its eyelids are held open, so that the light flashes can be perceived by the sight cells. After each flash the brain produces a weak electrical impulse that causes fluctuations on a screen.

How old is it?

The cat?

Yes, the cat.

They are six months old when they are used for experiments. As a matter of fact, this young lady has prepared a place for them in the basement. So they are always on hand.

The woman smiles. One nods. Then she covers up the cat's left eye, and the fluctuation on the screen is diminished. Does one eye give a weaker impulse than two? Or are the electrodes different in each division of the brain? One shifts one's eyes from the screen to the cat. It is breathing regularly. It is unreal that the animal with the fixed, staring eyes is breathing. But it is – for a few hours more.

Anyway, forget it.

Professor Warden's office is small and crammed with litter. On a corner of the desk stands an electric kettle. Dust floats up in the cup when the tea is poured.

My sister must have mentioned that Sebastian was very unusual. But she is too young to understand him and wasn't close to him, besides.

The professor leans back.

If I'd been able to strap him down in there – naturally on a larger table than the one for the cat – there would certainly have been very interesting fluctuations. Though we still know too little, unfortunately, about the neurological basis of the characteristics of my brother, whom you are going to write about. I'm not thinking of his hairless skin but of his behaviour. His natural talent, if you prefer.

One of my students, as a matter of fact, is working on an experiment that will perhaps bring us closer to an answer. It reminds one of the experiment with the cat, but here we have placed some brain cells in liquid nutritive. They receive small electric shocks and answer with discharges. There is a kind of electronic dialogue. It was a colleague's bequest that gave us the opportunity to carry this out. In a sense one can say that he has acquired a life after death.

But Sebastian's talent was of an entirely different kind, marked by fantasy and fearlessness. Therefore it would have been more difficult to localize in a definite sector of the brain.

The professor pours more tea.

Unasked, one thinks.

You should have seen him amuse himself terrifying villagers over there in Malaysia by flying low over the houses – making chickens, pigs and youngsters jump in all directions. Learning to control that little sports plane was dead easy for him. In spite of everything, the rest of us took some weeks to become familiar with the machine, but he was like a young eagle that just stretches its wings out and lifts off! In that way, too, he was success's carefree child.

Professor Warden smiles. Is it the memory of Sebastian, who – almost – could just stretch out his arms and fly? Or is it the thought of what the fluctuations on the screen might have shown, if he had managed to place the boy's brain cells between electrodes in a bowl of liquid nutritive?

The smile is irritating. Because it concerns only the one who smiles. But one is spared nearness. One looks openly at the clock in case one can make the night plane.

The professor stares at one motionlessly.

Like the cat, one thinks.

I've never mentioned this to anyone, but as you're writing about Sebastian, you ought to know it. He was a spy. Whom he spied for, I haven't a clue. That's unimportant, really. If you ask for proof, I can only say that I know. He couldn't have been anything else. Handsome, ageless, almost as much woman as man – daring and with a rare control of his body. With an adult's intelligence, besides, and a child's lack of morals.

Do I shock you by disclosing my view of the child and by revealing a dead brother's amoral occupation?

One thinks: Good God, what does he imagine?

As an author you ought to know that children don't have morals, but loyalties. Which are the opposite. Morals presuppose norms, loyalties, someone to look up to. Animals and children don't have norms, but can be loyal. A dog can go to his death for you, not because it has any conception of good and evil, but because of an impulsive attachment. This also applies to children. For this reason they are perfect soldiers. Only with adults can conflict arise between moral values and loyalty.

In that way, Sebastian was a child. He did everything for the one he admired. For example, me. When young, I carried out an experiment precisely to see if he was moral or loyal. Once at our country house in Provence I asked him to seduce Penelope, who was having tea with our grandmother. Because it involved a sister while the grandmother looked on, it was an expression of moral want. But because I said what it would mean to me to see Penny be seduced, he did it without misgiving.

I still have my notes on it.

There is something else I haven't mentioned either, which may be of importance during your preliminary work on the book. I was to blame for Sebastian's suicide.

One explains clearly that one is not engaged in any preliminary work.

The professor looks at one. Past one? Continues: You know that I was like a father to him. It had nothing to do with age, but with admiration. Even if he was absent-minded, he always listened attentively to me. It's possible, therefore, that I should have been more careful about experimenting to learn to what extent he took me at my word. There are thoughts which arise, but which a research scholar learns to see in a wider perspective.

To be sure, I can catch myself feeling sorrow when I picture him before the mirror surrounded by candles. With the camera pointed towards him, he raises the pistol and shoots. But with that we became witness to the experiment called death. Do you find that improper?

Surely he must understand that one is merely tired!

I once said that suicide is the ultimate proof of thought and separates the men from the beasts more than anything else. Animals can't imagine death. Therefore they don't take their own lives. As already mentioned, I should have been more careful, but wanted to see if, in his admiration for me, he would go still further than seducing his sister at afternoon tea.

The silence when the professor suddenly isn't speaking is frightening.

It is as if he has no words. Or thoughts. Or life. Nevertheless he takes his cup, stirs the tea slowly and drinks.

It's got cold!

One shrugs.

It's good, says the professor, that you undertook the commission. I said that Sebastian was a spy. Forget it. The most important thing is that he was unusual.

As one rises to leave, the professor mentions, as if it suddenly occurs to him: You must speak to George Barkley, the solicitor who arranged everything then. Splendid man. Travelled to Singapore the minute Sebastian's girl-friend had problems. Would have been damned annoying if they'd decided she killed him. For all of us. Homicide sets in motion so many unpleasant thoughts. Don't you agree?

One could barely listen to him.

As a matter of fact, I've arranged a meeting with Barkley for you. Unfortunately, he's in court all day, so you can't see him till tomorrow evening. Hope that's not inconvenient.

Inconvenient! one thinks.

Here's a card with name, address and time. He lives close to the hotel where I've booked a room for you. I thought it was just as simple for me to arrange it that way.

One puts the card in one's pocket without looking at it.

The Murder

Light is seeping in between the curtains and the window-sill, and it is still nine hours until the meeting with the solicitor. One can remain in bed or get up and sit in the chair by the television set.

It was turned on the evening before, when one arrived. One didn't see if it was the news or a film. It was a matter of complete indifference. The set had to go! But then someone would come to carry it out. So one turned the screen to the wall and pulled out the plug.

One refused Warden's proposal to have breakfast with him. Even the person who awakens one, draws back the curtains and says something about the weather deprives one of all appetite. One asks for the tray to be placed outside the door, so that no one will knock. A newspaper lies beside the rolls, marmalade and tea. One flings it in front of the door across the hall.

The noise increases in the street outside. Consciousness of the swarm of people there makes further sleep impossible. Constantly importunate, insignificant faces. Most of them loathsome, but some reminiscent of the image one has formed of Sebastian. He looks at one. Expressionless, demanding.

He has no right to demand anything of one. He is dead. Why does one let a dead person press into one's mind? What is it that makes one lie in a half-dark room in a strange city and wait for an unknown solicitor to tell one something one doesn't want to know?

Lies nevertheless and waits.

Longing for the harbour and the glass of pastis becomes overpower-
ing. The harbour is out of reach, but the pastis? One reaches for the
telephone. Hesitates. For it isn't the pastis but a world without an
outside world one is longing for. Like a pain. Or more accurately, the
outside world is the pain.

After a while, one thinks: Why go to the meeting about Sebastian?
Why not just get up, pack and take the first plane back to the harbour
and the glass of pastis?

And so one gets up, opens one's suitcase and puts in what one has
brought along. A shirt, a pair of socks, pyjamas, toilet articles,
shaver. It is not enough to keep from moving, even if one tightens the
straps. So one straightens up and looks to see if one has forgotten
anything. One's reading-glasses lie on the bedside table. They don't
go into the case but into one's jacket pocket.

Then everything must be in order.

But again the image of Sebastian stands before one. One also hears
Rose Mayfield recount what the doctors said when they came with his
heart: How handsome he was! Why did *he* take his own life?

How does that concern one? one thought then.

One still thinks that, now with more bitterness than indifference.
The journey, the professor, the solicitor belong to the world outside
the world one has created for oneself. How can people assume as a
matter of course that one will write about a person one would
probably never have wanted to know?

Nevertheless one doesn't pick up the suitcase and leave the room.
Without understanding it, actually without thinking, one lies down on
the bed, kicks off one's shoes and closes one's eyes as if to sleep.

Eventually, it begins to grow dark. One has lain there sleeping all day
long. Although, whether one slept or not, nothing took place inside
one. One just lay and waited. Waited to get the meeting over, so that

one could sit down in a plane and return to the house behind the garden wall.

At last it has become so dark that one must turn the light on to see the clock. It's time. One puts on one's shoes, hangs one's overcoat over one's arm and leaves the hotel.

Mr Barkley, the solicitor, opens the outer door himself. Not until he has led the way into his library does he express regret – but in a voice that discloses it doesn't trouble him in the slightest – that it has been impossible for him to see one before. In the same voice, he asks if one would like something to drink, and pours two glasses of wine without waiting for an answer.

As far as I understood Professor Warden, you wish to see me because you are writing a book about his dead brother Sebastian.

One mumbles to oneself: No book's being written.

It was an interesting case. Of course I knew Sebastian only quite superficially, but when his father rang up about the tragedy and mentioned that the police were in doubt about the cause of death, I naturally travelled to Singapore immediately.

He suddenly interrupts himself: How thoughtless of me – won't you sit down? The chairs here by the fire are very comfortable, so if you have no objection. . . .

He sits down and continues: As I'm sure you realize, the death took place at the family's country house and in what one may call special circumstances. Now, one can naturally say that all deaths not caused by age or illness do so. But this was – if you will allow me the expression – staged in a somewhat strange manner. Not the least strange features were the mirror that was hung up for the occasion, the candles and the aria 'Remember me' from Purcell's *Dido and Aeneas* sung by Kathleen Ferrier at full volume on the house stereo system. Then too, the camera to immortalize the moment of death.

Again he interrupts himself: Won't you really sit down?

One hesitates. Not that one likes to stand, but the armchair seems like a trap. A spider's web spun from that chilly account. Besides, one feels – to one's surprise – a distaste because of the bizarre details.

But it isn't the bizarre in itself that awakens the distaste; it is the thought that, some day, these people will come to concern one. Nevertheless one sits down.

It was, continues the solicitor after sipping his wine, undoubtedly staged. But by whom? Sebastian wasn't alone, you know. An old Chinese servant lived at the country house, and that evening Sebastian had a visit from a girl named June Wong. Like so many of his lady-friends, she was a dubious acquaintance whom no one knew anything about. A lack of expression is characteristic of the race, but I was put off by the fact that her face looked like carved ivory even when she was arrested.

One hears oneself ask: Was she indicted for Sebastian's murder? No, arrested. And with good reason. If one leaves the servant out of account, she was alone with him. He always had a great deal of money on him, and her fingerprints were on the weapon. She said she unconsciously put the pistol on a table when she found him, and she rang for a doctor. But what else could she have said? The servant appeared as soon as he heard the shot.

One is going to ask if the girl was in the room when the servant arrived, but checks oneself. As if one has nevertheless asked, the solicitor says: At first, the old man said that June was sitting with the pistol in her hand when he arrived. However, he changed his statement and claimed that she ran ahead of him, threw herself down by Sebastian and seized the pistol.

The solicitor leans back and sips his wine again. Then he says: Ah, but you aren't drinking. Don't you like wine?

One raises one's glass and drinks.

Of course I didn't think for a moment that anyone would accept the servant's new explanation. Suicide releases feelings of guilt and anxiety because of what others think. A murder committed by a girl like June Wong causes no such speculations. At worst, one could have imagined it as a matter of jealousy. At best, a matter of money.

But as early as the day after, the police accepted the new explanation. It also received the family's support. The old man had been with them for years. He could become confused in a crisis, but once he calmed down, he was entirely reliable. They also stood up for the girl – said that she and Sebastian had been extremely close to each other, and that she couldn't possibly have caused his death.

As the family's solicitor, I rejected the explanation and said that the whole business was staged. Everything from the mirror to the aria was supposed to give the impression of suicide as a demonstration or public protest. The camera was supposed to provide proof. But it failed to work.

As an author, you almost certainly have some profound explanation or other. But I'm accustomed to the practical life. At first I assumed that the police wanted to protect their countrymen. I also thought that the family wanted to spare two people who had perhaps meant much to Sebastian. Then I met a Chinese colleague who hinted, with apparent casualness, that the Wardens had bribed a high-ranking police officer to avert the prosecution of June Wong.

George Barkley leans back again in his chair. This time he empties his glass as a sign that he has ended the story. That there is no more to say about events in Singapore.

One doesn't delay in getting up.

But the solicitor picks up an envelope.

If I'd been writing about Sebastian, I'd have visited June Wong. She may have something to tell. Here's the address she was at then.

Resigned, one takes the envelope and leaves. In the weak light one can only just see one's wrist-watch. Far too many wasted hours.

Fortunately, the departure lounges at Heathrow are virtually empty of people. Some elderly Indians are sweeping up paper and cigarette-ends. It has no significance. They take no notice of one; one is as invisible as they are. If one lifts one's legs so that an Indian can reach under with his brush, they rise as if by themselves.

When day dawns, the morning plane leaves.

The dog is sitting at the gate when one has finally mounted the steep hill from the harbour. But it doesn't look at one. It merely follows one through the gate and the front door. For a brief second, something happens with one hand. As if it will stretch itself out towards the animal.

It must be imagination.

Note about a Journey

The thought of June Wong is disturbing. Even when one is drinking pastis at the harbour, a voice one doesn't want to hear is asking: What kind of a woman was she?

One puts the glass down and walks to the house. But she follows. One catches oneself talking to the dog. If it looks at one, the image of June disappears. If it lowers its head, the image returns. Beautiful image. One knows only that she is Chinese. Does one believe that she is attractive because Sebastian was?

At night one thinks about what the solicitor thought June Wong could reveal. For the first time one calls the dog. It stops a short distance from the bed. In the darkness, the only thing visible is the eyes, which mirror the moonlight. They observe one. Questioningly? Then they are gone.

This person! The only thing one wants to think about is if the weather is good enough for a walk down to the harbour for a glass of pastis.

Although it is meaningless, one travels to Singapore one morning. Where one has never wanted to go. So that one can sit in peace at the harbour afterwards and watch the women making their purchases.

As they do every day.

On the journey one sleeps. One scarcely notices where the stops are. Dubai? Bangkok? When the plane comes in to land at Changi Airport, one perceives that people are stretching to catch a glimpse of Singapore. Is there anything to see? Parks, skyscrapers and slums. Like everywhere else in the world.

Besides, it is probably too late to see anything but the lights. One hasn't looked at one's watch. One will learn soon enough how dark it is when one disembarks.

One must wait until the next day to look for June Wong and asks the taxi-driver to take one to a hotel. The driver looks at one in the mirror. One seems to recall that the founder was called Raffles, and believes that a street is called after him.

Something or other Raffles Street.

The cabby drives to a hotel in Orchard Road. One doesn't notice the name. In the room, one pulls out the plug of the television set and asks for food to be left outside the door. It is hot, so one undresses before one eats. Barely tastes what. After returning the tray to the corridor, one lies down.

At daybreak, it is still hot. It is also humid. One's clothes stick to one's body. But one dresses and walks down to reception, where two Chinese porters greet one with formal effusiveness. One scarcely nods as one shows them the card one got from Mr Barkley.

They speak Chinese in a low voice. Then they bow and say that it is in Tua Poh. They have ordered a taxi. One leans back in the taxi and closes one's eyes. The driver asks if it is one's first time in Singapore. One doesn't answer.

The traffic noises are succeeded by cries in a language one doesn't understand. The street is as one might have imagined it – cramped, with clothes hung out to dry on poles and children that stretch out their hands for money when the taxi stops. One doesn't even look at them.

After receiving his fare, the taxi-driver hesitates. Then he brings one into a courtyard. It too is the way one might have imagined it. Chickens, pigs and half-naked youngsters all mixed up together. Some old people are sitting on a flight of steps, and a younger woman is cooking food under a tin roof.

One stands while the driver speaks to the old ones. A little girl comes with a chicken in her arms. To show it to one? A gift? One pushes her away. The woman under the tin roof smiles cautiously. Two of her front teeth are missing. One looks at the driver impatiently. Finally, he comes running, smiles.

June Wong lives here, but works in Jurong bird sanctuary. You can come back here this evening if you want to meet her.

Drive to Jurong!

One tries to sleep in the back seat. The heat is intolerable when the driver stops, and, wet through, one leaves one's jacket behind in the taxi.

To find June Wong, one must take the driver with one into the sanctuary. As if friends on an outing. In high spirits, he shows one the small ponds and artificial waterfalls. Stops to point at cockatoos, Persian nightingales and flamingos. As if one has never seen birds before!

One doesn't stop. The driver comes running and calls out that one is going the wrong way. That June Wong works in the cafeteria by the cooled pond with the penguins. As if one knows where that is. On reaching the tables, he whispers: To sit down, we must eat.

One sighs.

Order anything.

The driver bows and runs to the counter. Why does he have to run all the time? One looks at the serving staff. Young women, frightfully alike. Who can be June Wong? Then the taxi-driver comes smiling to the table with one of them.

She isn't as pretty as one supposed. As if to give one time, she changes the cloth and slowly lays the table, but doesn't look at one. One doesn't manage to say anything. After that ghastly long journey, one doesn't know what one should say! Uneasily, one thinks that one can ask why she gave the picture of Sebastian to Rose Mayfield that night at the hospital.

Not a flicker passes over her face. Didn't she hear one? Didn't one manage to say it? Carefully, she straightens the cutlery. As it was crooked. Turns the plate a bit, to get the pattern with its blue birds in proper alignment with the guest.

Then June Wong says in a low voice: Sebastian came to live in the dying woman. She had to learn who he was, he who was within her insignificant body.

What was Sebastian like?

Then she looks at one, coolly.

A human being. Quite different from what his family saw. Wanted to see. They tried to buy him, the way they tried to buy me. As they've bought you to write the book about him. They believe they can get everything for money, even your innermost thoughts. Your self. But he had the vision of a child, so he saw what they were trying to do. That they wanted to prevent him from fighting for the weak and oppressed.

Sebastian – fighting for the oppressed?

One sees a hint of a smile.

They haven't told you that, I'm sure. That he travelled to the villages, that he spoke to the poor people no one will admit exist. Said they mustn't acquire colour television, but knowledge. Power. That's how we met. In a backyard in Tua Poh. He told us how the prime minister Lee Kuan Yew exploits the weak. He was like a young god.

Not Penelope's naked Pan, one thinks.

The smile, if it was a smile, is gone. She moves the glasses slightly. Restlessly. As if she mustn't waste time talking to the guests. Straightens up and says quickly: If you want the truth about the Warden family, go and see Arthur Cunningham on Raffles Quay. Don't say I've sent you.

Then she is gone.

One should never have met June Wong. When she walked away, she turned and looked at one. What did her eyes speak of? Of hate? Sorrow? No one else who talked about Sebastian had that look. One fears it will be impossible to forget it. At the harbour one will see it coming from the black-clad women. Even the dark eyes of the dog will be changed into hers. An animal can't weep. In the taxi one sees before one the tears moisten the grey-brown fur.

That dog must leave the house!

One asked the driver to go to Changi in order to make the afternoon plane. He simply swung out from the place in front of the bird sanctuary. One closes one's eyes and tries not to think of June Wong, the toothless woman, the children's outstretched hands.

The taxi stops suddenly.

But this isn't Changi Airport!

No, Raffles Quay.

Neither moves or says anything. A silent test of strength ensues. One feels a bewildering uneasiness. What does the man want?

Talk to Mr Cunningham!

One feels uncertain, gropes.

Did you know Sebastian, too?

Ask him about the old servant.

Arthur Cunningham sits with his back to a window overlooking the large harbour. He leans back in the leather chair at his desk, folds his hands behind his neck and looks at one. He is used to looking at people. He likes it.

So that's what you look like.

He smiles and continues: To tell you the truth, I was expecting you. When a little bird told me that someone had undertaken to write a book about poor Sebastian, I thought to myself: Sooner or later he'll come to me.

There isn't any commission.

Cleverly stated! One mustn't commit oneself until all the cards are on the table. But now I'm keen to know what you intend to ask me.

One feels distaste. The figure leaning back with its hands folded behind its neck. The white silk shirt with a monogram. The view that makes the people down there look like insignificant insects. It is the taxi-driver's fault that one is here. What was it he said when one got out of the taxi? Something about the old servant?

Mr Cunningham straightens up. Places his hands on the desk. Only a vase of flowers is standing there. Smiles no more.

I'm sure you'll have something to drink.

Fills two glasses with gin and bitters. Adds ice. Pushes one glass towards the middle of the table, so that one must get up to take it.

He leans back in his chair again.

Whatever people have said about the old man, it's only rumours. A journalist – I've preferred to forget who – wrote after the tragedy that the servant had been paid to shoot Sebastian. The reason was supposed to have been that the boy was looked on as an agitator by some. Which is nonsense. He was a playboy, not a reformer. To him, the destitute were picturesque walk-ons.

Where is the old man now?

Mr Cunningham pushes his glass away.

Singapore is a well-ordered community. No one pays for murders. True enough, Sebastian had a . . . let me call her girl-friend. She probably killed him. Not for payment but from hate.

Yet again he leans back.

Such people believe that the one who has money has everything. But take the Warden family, now, scattered to the four winds. They belonged to each other through Sebastian. Now he's gone because an ignorant chit of a girl saw this innocent child as an expression of a prosperity she herself didn't have. Because she didn't understand that money isn't happiness but responsibility.

On the way to the airport one thinks: Has this man ever been in the backyards, experienced the outstretched hands? Why did they want one to talk to him? One closes one's eyes again, tries not to think. It has become more difficult. Through the din of the traffic one hears June Wong's voice. Through one's eyelids one sees Sebastian. Whom one has never met.

Was that why they wanted it?

Dialogue in the Night

The dog isn't standing at the gate to the house. Although it is late in the evening and dark, one would have seen it even at a distance. Has one become dependent on a creature one hardly knows?

One will forget it. Hears oneself say: It's the dog's affair whether it is there or not! Nevertheless one looks towards the fireplace when one has let oneself in. Dead tired, one doesn't unpack. Doesn't eat, doesn't wash, just strips off one's clothes and falls heavily on to the bed.

One doesn't sleep, but catches oneself listening in the darkness. Wasn't that whining outside the front door? But one has never heard the dog whine. Again one gives a start because something sounds like whimpering. Or is it a faint yelping noise, as when the dog is dreaming? But it's nothing.

Suddenly one sits up in the bed, confused. One must have slept all the same. Distantly, one perceives that there is a faint knocking on the front door. Did one wake up because someone has been standing there knocking?

One puts on one's trousers, pulls a shirt over one's head and goes out barefoot to open the door. It is cold on the flagstone floor.

A young woman is standing outside in the moonlight one thinks it is Penelope Warden, who wrote the letter and asked if she might visit one. Dark skin, black hair, a slender figure. Then one sees that the

49

skin is more grey than dark, that the hair is short, and that she isn't slender but thin. Penelope's pale shadow.

She says, softly and without expression: You've been to Singapore. One lets one's glance glide through her, past her. Looks out into the garden for the dog. Strangely, it is nowhere.

And what then?

You spoke to June about Sebastian's death?

It's the middle of the night!

I've waited all day.

Without a word, one goes in. Hears her following one. Did she leave the door open? In the living-room, one lights the lamp and throws oneself down in a chair. Doesn't ask her to sit down, and she remains standing. One realizes that it must be a sister of Penelope and Sebastian, but can't remember any name. Doesn't want to know it, either.

I'm Camilla, she says. Camilla Warden.

One stiffens. Ignores it.

I've learnt that you're working on a book about Sebastian. In that case, you must hear the truth. That's why I've come.

One stands up. Not suddenly, but slowly. Feels that one is transformed into wordless rage. These people take it for granted that one has taken on this commission! A rage that must have been inside one for a long time, but just hadn't congealed into expression. For she is standing there, this pale woman, and saying one must hear the truth. The way they all do! One feels rage in every muscle. In every cell.

One observes as at a distance how one lays hold of the woman and lifts her up. One carries her without feeling the weight of that thin, but nevertheless grown, person and throws her out through the front door.

She lies there motionless. But not because she is injured. It seems like a submission, a posture of beseeching. One is going to slam the door shut again, but her eyes stop one. One rages at the power of her submission, leaves the door as it is and goes back into the living-room.

One sits down there and waits as if for the dog. For her to come crawling. She comes, but not on all fours. She merges into the wall, says nothing. Again one is roused to indignation, this time at the power of her silence. Which will force one to speak. Finally, one asks: What is the truth about Sebastian?

She detaches herself from the wall. Becomes calm, becomes stronger. One thinks: Does she believe she has won? Is that the way she is accustomed to win? With submission and silence? One turns away to avoid seeing the suspicion of a smile on those thin lips.

One hears her say in a soft voice: Sebastian was worshipped. When he appeared at our home, my grandmother became excited. Fetch the wine, Camilla! Bring the chocolates here! Put out a chair, so Sebastian can sit beside me! As if he couldn't do such a thing himself.

Again one sees the suspicion of a smile.

No one paid any attention to me, except when something had to be done. But I stayed in there with them. At a distance! Sometimes he looked at me. Grandmother never noticed it. He wanted to remind me that we had a secret together.

Did you?

The question just slipped out of one. One doesn't want to know anything at all. But it is too late. First she bows her head, then she looks directly at one.

We did. He visited me at night without Grandmother having any suspicion of it. Came silently into my room and took the covers off me. I lay there completely naked. He never touched me. He just sat and looked at me while he told me I was more beautiful than any of the women he had slept with. Even June, the Chinese girl you saw in Singapore. That it was meaningless and empty. I know I'm not beautiful. But as I lay there in the half-light, my body took on a loveliness it doesn't have.

She smiles.

Sebastian gave me that. Some nights I thought I should bring him in to me. That he came for that reason. But I didn't dare to. If I had yielded, what happened would perhaps never have happened. No, I *know* it wouldn't have happened.

Know?

She becomes restless, looks away.

Don't ask me how, but I know that he would never have shot himself if he hadn't felt that the emptiness was unbearable. His face on those nights! That wonderfully beautiful face. Even sorrow can be beautiful. I knew he was going to do it.

Without forewarning, she sinks down on to her knees. One feels her head in one's lap and stiffens. Wants to push her away, but fears that any touch may seem like concern. So one keeps one's hands as far away from her as possible. Her face rests against one's thighs, her fingers bore into one. But one feels absolutely nothing.

One shouts: Get up, get up!

She doesn't move. Slowly, a warmth beneath her face and fingers is felt. One tries to edge backwards in one's chair. It is impossible. The chair is a trap. One thinks: She will lay the body bare. Aloud, one says: For God's sake, Camilla, get up!

She remains motionless. But she looks at one. Is it because one thoughtlessly spoke her name? Her look is beseeching in its self-effacement. It makes one uneasy, and one tries to avoid it. One feels her straighten up, and as one unwillingly looks at her, with no expression on her face, she takes off her dress. Absently, one thinks: Why has she nothing underneath, except a necklace with a little cross? Does she go about like that, or is it because she had this in mind?

She is more beautiful than one imagined. Though one hasn't imagined anything. She is not so thin. Even in the half-light – or maybe because of it – her body has a golden sheen that her face lacks. One thinks that she must neither lean against one nor smile.

This is how Sebastian saw me.

One nods, says softly: You must get dressed again.

She makes no sign of putting on her dress, but sits as if paralysed. The only life one is aware of is her breathing. Her breast that rises and falls.

Then one shouts: Get dressed and go!

One might just as well have struck her. But a moment later she is sitting as before. With one difference. Her eyes are filled with tears. Nothing betrays that she is aware of it, but she is crying. Without a movement in her face, without a sound. One says nothing, doesn't stretch out one's hand to stroke her cheek. Just looks on – and waits.
Where shall I go?
She says that to herself. A spoken thought that requires no answer. One sees that she has become a child instead of a woman. Sees it with anxiety, for one does not want to be misled into caring about a person one has nothing to do with. Who comes uninvited in the middle of the night. Why doesn't she put her dress on?
Nevertheless one asks: Haven't you booked anywhere?
She shakes her head.
Haven't you anything with you?
No. I just set out when I heard you were writing about Sebastian. I couldn't bring anything with me, so no one could know where I was going. Then they'd have prevented me from saying what he was like.

One is going to say that none of this concerns one. Then one becomes aware of a shadow in the doorway. The dog. Is one moved? Stretches, for the first time, a hand out towards it. It doesn't see it, but walks over to the woman. It stands there a moment, then lies down with its head in her lap.
If one had given it a thought, one would have believed that she had become frightened. But she puts her arms round the dog, calmly, as if she has expected it. Cautiously, it licks her on the neck. She whispers something. It sounds like a name.

One stands up. She doesn't notice it as she sits there holding the animal. It is like a painting from the last century. The moonlight in through the window, the nude woman on the floor, the dog's head

resting on one of her thighs. One thinks: The dog has guided her to
the closed room within herself. She is no longer beseeching, submissive. Did she become like that when Sebastian came to her in her
grandmother's house?

One hears oneself say: You can sleep here tonight.

She doesn't notice that, either. Again one thinks of the painting.
The room is a clearing in the woods. Pan is with her. Or perhaps
Sebastian in the form of an animal.

One has lain down on the bed. One has left the door ajar. Is one
waiting for the dog? Or for the young woman? One is unable to sleep.
The whole time one imagines the two in the room next door. They
are sleeping as if in a meadow, sleeping close together to keep warm
in the summer night.

Why has she come – Camilla Warden? She said it was to tell one
the truth about Sebastian. But the only thing she told one was about
his visits to their grandmother's. About when she was the unnoticed
one who served wine and chocolates, and when she let Sebastian sit
and see her naked. She was talking about herself.

Perhaps that's what we always do, one thinks. Though she must
have passed on something about her brother. One can't stop seeing
him there, sitting by her bed: lonely among his conquests, helpless in
his success.

Was that her truth about Sebastian?

The Shipwreck

When one awakens, the dog and Camilla are gone. On the oak table lies a sheet of paper with two questions written on it. The handwriting reminds one of Penelope's, but slants helplessly down the paper.

Why was Sebastian in Singapore?

What do you know about my family?

One crumples up the sheet, throws it in the fireplace and tries to forget what was on it. One would have undoubtedly managed to do so, if one had not already put the same questions to oneself. Imprudently enough, one has even tried to have them answered.

From a letter to James R. Henderson at Henderson East Asian Line, London:

As you may possibly recall, you travelled some years ago from Paris to Ajaccio by plane, during which journey you spoke of interesting experiences in Lebanon. Upon arrival at Ajaccio, you graciously suggested that one might write to you, if one, as a writer, required information about shipping.

You must excuse the fact that what you now are being asked about is undoubtedly on the borderline of what you then had in mind. It concerns Richard Warden, with whom you are perhaps acquainted, as he is also a shipowner.

A daughter of his has, on behalf of the family, requested that a

55

book be written about his son Sebastian, who died in tragic circumstances in Singapore. Naturally, one can't undertake such a
commission, but the tragedy has not failed to make a certain
impression. Moreover, it is strange that one wants to have a book
written about a man who accomplished hardly anything.

The few pieces of information at hand make it reasonable to
believe that the family must be fairly unusual. The behaviour of the
son, living almost alone in Singapore, is also somewhat strange, con-
sidering that the family as a rule live in England or on the Riviera.

If it is not too much trouble, it would be interesting if you could
provide some supplementary information about the Wardens.
Then, possibly, the consequences for the members of the family of
one's being unable to undertake the commission will be clearer.

What caused one to write the letter is in itself impossible to understand. Probably one did it to pass the time one day when one's trip to
the harbour was prevented by bad weather. But that one posted it is
incomprehensible. After all, one must have known that the danger of
a reply from a man like James R. Henderson was imminent.

One forgot, of course, that one had even sent it.

But one day the postman knocked on the door. The post-box had
long since rusted to pieces, and one saw no reason to put up a new
one. Nothing would ever arrive that could be placed in it.

One realized that it was the answer, but barely looked through it.
Why let oneself be lumbered with a letter about a family that doesn't
concern one? It must have been something about James R. Henderson's courtesy that restrained one from throwing it away. One had
put it somewhere or other. Where?

One had forgotten that, too.

Irritated by what the apparently submissive Camilla Warden makes
one do, one begins to search. There aren't many possibilities. A pile
of unimportant papers on the oak table, an old cupboard and some
drawers in a chest. One finds it serving as a bookmark in one of the
books by the bed.

Extract from the reply from James R. Henderson of Henderson East Asian Line, London:

And so to the Wardens. I don't know whether you have been told, but the shipping company in which Richard Warden has earned his money was founded in England by his father and had its head office in London until recently. Old Warden was a serious man of Scandinavian ancestry. In its first years, the shipping company wasn't large but thoroughly solid. During the First World War it grew considerably, and in the inter-war years it strengthened its position by transporting general cargo in small ships. These very ships were very successful during the Second World War and led to further growth.

Old Warden died at the end of the fifties, and Richard took over the management of the company. The difference between father and son gradually became clear. The elder Warden was a man who preferred small and safe seas, to use an obvious image. The son wanted to be a big success. Not long after the father's death, he began to gamble on tanker shipping and had ships built that were among the largest in the world. Even if the market was promising, such measures demanded not only daring but also very high loans. While the father would scarcely have had a peaceful night, with crises constantly looming up like dark clouds on the horizon, the son obviously enjoyed balancing on a knife-edge.

Then one day in the seventies something happened. The company's largest ship, *Warden Giant*, was quite simply lost on the way from Indonesia to South Africa, reportedly with crude oil. You remember it, I'm sure, for the world press was full of the matter for weeks. Not only was it sensational that a ship so large simply disappeared without leaving the slightest trace, but the amount of the insurance for the ship and her cargo was moreover so high that even people at Lloyd's became uneasy.

The theories about the accident were numerous and elaborate. Because neither oil slicks, pieces of wreckage nor survivors had been found, some even began to doubt whether any shipwreck had taken place. One could have stopped, after all, to report the position, and that way people would know that the ship had vanished. Others thought that she had been the target of sabotage or captured by black Africans, since she was heading for South

Africa with oil. The more technically knowledgeable thought that
the tanker had been exposed to a rare kind of very long and
powerful wave. The hull might then have been lifted fore and aft,
and the length of the span between the wave tops could have
caused her to break in two. But in that case, apparently, oil would
have leaked out. If there was oil on board. One theory, you see,
held that the oil cargo was a bluff to collect the very sizeable
insurance money. Without having the details clearly before me, I
seem to remember that they found irregularities with regard to the
shipping of the oil – something that isn't unusual where oil cargoes
for South Africa are concerned. If the ship wasn't loaded with
crude oil, there was, moreover, the possibility of an explosion,
which can be caused by oil vapour in empty tankers.

After an unbelievably long time, they found a life-raft in the
Indian Ocean. It clearly came from *Warden Giant*. There was a
man on board, half dead from thirst and mentally injured by the
stress. It was impossible to get anything sensible out of him.
Instead, he talked as if in a trance about a violent storm with
lightning and thunder. When *Warden Giant* vanished, however,
there was no storm in those waters. So it's either a question of a
storm he had experienced earlier or of explosions that he, with his
confused mind, remembered as flickering lightning and crashing
thunder.

The maritime enquiry was virtually an impossibility, but it was
held. The mentally injured man's account of the storm was pro-
duced as evidence that in any case something had happened to the
ship, and that she had gone to the bottom for that reason. So the
insurance money for both ship and cargo was reluctantly paid at
last.

With that, the matter was formally settled and done with. For
Richard, however, it became a still greater burden in an unexpected way. Before the settlement, both his family and his colleagues were clearly on his side, but after the insurance companies
had agreed that the ship was lost, even the members of his family
became both evasive and suspicious. The whole thing was too
convenient. Hadn't the finances been critical because of large loans
and depressed times? Would such a violent explosion have occurred if the tanks had been filled with crude oil? Could the
confused sailor really have come from *Warden Giant*?

Old Wilhelm Warden, the shipping firm's founder, was recognized by everyone as the personification of integrity, and the family saw it as an obligation to carry on this heritage. The least offence, even a parking infringement, was seen as a moral stain. While other people would have regarded the results of the maritime enquiry as a stroke of luck in a difficult economic situation, it was precisely its convenience that was felt to be doubtful. Decent toil, not successful speculations, and above all not manipulations on the frontiers of the law, was looked on as the only respectable basis for growth and progress.

For Richard this became intolerable. True enough, nothing dramatic ever occurred. But the family's behaviour was marked by an aloofness – a rejection. At last Richard and his wife separated, the other members of the family were bought out, and the operations were moved from London to Singapore.

Naturally I have no knowledge of what happened inside the four walls of the house. It is possible, however, that Bob Ridgway, a young man who seemed to be a close friend of Sebastian's, has something to tell. As a matter of form, I have taken the liberty of sending him a hint that you will possibly get in touch with him.

One flings the letter on the table and thinks that one should never have read it. Several times one felt a desire to see other members of the Warden family. Unwished for questions also broke surface. Was it the family's aloofness or Richard's own feeling of guilt that drove him to Singapore? Do morality and guilt lie behind the need to have the book about Sebastian written? Can the lively Bob, who was in charge of the video recording after the funeral, really have something substantial to tell?

It has grown too late to go down to the harbour. Being at home in the morning, one makes an exception and pours out a glass of pastis, sits down at the fireplace, where the dog usually lies, and drinks very slowly.

But the questions don't go away.

Dialogue about a Model

The only place Sebastian releases one now is the harbour. The fishing-boats that have come in with the morning's catch of squid, the black-clad women who have made their purchases, and the glass of pastis that stands in front of one on the round café table erase consciousness. The all-overshadowing moment abolishes it.

Though when one has hesitantly called to the dog during the night, and it comes in to one and stands there by the bed, Sebastian also disappears. Then there are only the eyes that mirror the moonlight. One night, the animal laid its head on the bedspread. Waiting. Unconsciously, one stretched out one's hand and stroked the soft cheek, and a strange peace streamed through one. It felt frightening, degrading, and one withdrew one's hand, ashamed.

A shadow falls across the café table just as one is about to raise one's glass of pastis. It was cast by a young man in a white suit and a pink shirt. The collar is open, a narrow gold chain comes into view. Then one remembers. Some days previously the telephone rang. A man – one forgot immediately what he said he was called – referred to a letter from James R. Henderson and said he would very much like to visit one, with regard to the book about Sebastian. Would lunch-time on Tuesday be convenient?

One thinks: Is that now?

61

The young man bends towards one across the table and stretches out his hand.

I'm Bob Ridgway. A neighbour of yours said you usually sit down here at the harbour. I was the one who rang you on Sunday evening. If it's inconvenient, I'll be glad to come back another day.

One disregards the outstretched hand. Doesn't travel mean anything to these people? One sips from the glass, observes the man. Conceited or merely young? The man hesitates, uncertain of the situation. Then he sits down.

He smiles. Uneasily?

Penny has told me about the fantastic reception you gave her. About your repairing that old piece of jewellery. Are you sure I'm not disturbing you?

One doesn't answer.

When Jim wrote that you had turned to him about the Wardens, I thought I might as well take a trip, so you wouldn't be interrupted in your work on the book.

One sighs.

It's incredible that you sit on an island so like a Greek one and write about Sebastian. He was like a Hellenic youth, you know. An Orpheus. I keep wondering what Eurydice he crossed the Styx to fetch.

One puts the glass down on the round café table. Turns to face the fishing-boats.

Why must something be written about Sebastian?

The young man stares at one.

If you had met him, you wouldn't ask. Sebastian was a unique human being. He was a person everyone should read about as a model. Perhaps we didn't notice it when he was alive, but now we realize it. I myself saw only the Sebastian who was full of surprising, crazy ideas, not the one who humbly sacrificed himself – for instance, for the street-children.

One raises one's eyebrows.

You have a wrong impression of Sebastian. It's right, as far as it goes, that he could suddenly get into his sports plane and leave for Hong Kong or Bangkok and spend thousands of dollars on a holiday. He could also turn up at my place in New York and set a night-club completely on end. But during the day, when we thought he was sleeping, he sought out the street-children, the prostitute mothers in the slums, the poor blacks whom previously I hadn't regarded as people. Of course he never mentioned anything about it, but an endless number of these lost beings can thank Sebastian for the beginning of a new and worthier life.

One smiles faintly.

Bob Ridgway, as one remembers the young man is called, leans forward towards one. So that the words shall acquire greater weight? To arouse sympathy?

Sebastian's death changed my life. Before, it was without meaning. True enough, I studied at Yale. If I hadn't, I'd have had to go to work. Besides, you meet your own kind there – young girls you might marry some day. But I met Sebastian in New York as often as possible or went off to see him in Dakar or Singapore. Those black and those Asiatic women are fantastic.

Did Sebastian think so, too?

The young man says distinctly: There's something you must try to understand. Sebastian was a gentleman. He never slept with a woman without paying for it.

The harbour dozes in the sun. The black-clad women have gone home with their goods, some solitary fishermen sit on the boat-decks and mend tackle. One lets one's glance rest on the slowly working men and fixes one's attention on every little movement. Nevertheless one can't stop thinking about Bob Ridgway. The smooth face one avoids looking at. How did he manage it? Life at Yale with his 'own kind' – with the well-bred daughters of prosperous families – and the nights with coloured prostitutes in Dakar and Bangkok? With no transition but a one-day trip by plane?

Bob Ridgway smiles distantly: It's like flicking a switch.

The heat has also driven the fishermen away. There are only some children playing at the pier's edge in the shadow of an old maple. One fills the pastis glass while distantly noticing that young Bob Ridgway is drying his brow. Why doesn't he order something to drink? Does he expect one to serve him refreshments?

The young man breathes heavily.

You don't like me. You didn't believe me when I said that Sebastian's death changed my life. But it's true. I want to leave the university and look life in the eyes where it really exists. The way we now know Sebastian did. Maybe I don't have his strength, but Sebastian saw – of course in another connection – that strength is something you get by testing it, again and again. You're smiling at me? Well, go ahead. But I'll show the lot of you that I can live up to the model Sebastian has become for me.

One hears oneself mumble: It isn't a question of liking or not. You are a matter of complete unimportance. As Sebastian, his death and a book about him are. But with you sitting here like this, it is perhaps tempting to say: Live your own life, not Sebastian's, no matter how you think it was or might have been.

One regrets saying anything.

Though did he understand?

None of the Wardens understood Sebastian when he was alive. Even Penny, who visited you first, didn't see him as anything other than a handsome prince. A seductive, charming man who enjoyed life without thought for others. But that was only a role he played to conceal his despair over people's emptiness and distress. He played games to spare us the seriousness, because he knew that games were all that came natural to us.

Just let him talk!

When I saw him in his coffin in Singapore, it came to me for the first time how wrong we'd been about him. His face was no longer like a child's, but devastated by pain. The injustice, the starved children, the exploited prostitutes, the meaningless wars appeared in his anguished features. His lifeless eyes looked at me as if they were saying: I am the truth, the way you must go.

One reflects with resignation: Good God, was he another Christ?

That I don't know. I only knew that if my life was to have a meaning, I had to become like him. That is, the way he really was, not the way we'd always seen him – and which I was probably responsible for.

One turns to him. Responsible?

Bob Ridgway, the young man, had taken off his jacket without one's having noticed it. The sweat makes dark red stains on his pink shirt.

I've never told anyone this before, but it was I who took him along to the first woman he ever had. Once long ago in Bangkok. One had to find out if he was a man. Although she was just a child, she knew her profession. I'd made sure of that myself. But he remained just as ageless. Even after countless women, his skin was just as smooth and hairless. But of course we knew then that nothing was wrong with him. He was normal.

That was what made the greatest impression when I saw him in the coffin. His skin wasn't smooth any more. It came to me then for the first time that I'd never thought about how old he was. That he hadn't changed since the first time I saw him. It must have been at the family's estate in Provence. An old house where Sebastian grew up surrounded by big lawns and oak trees.

To understand him, one had to have been there!

The young man isn't sitting at the table any longer. Perhaps one has seen him go, even said a kind of farewell. Perhaps not. It is completely unimportant.

The essential thing is the harbour.

It must have grown late in the day. The fishermen are back on the decks of the boats, putting their tackle in place, setting out the crates for the next morning's catch of squid. Some have gone ashore and are wandering slowly under the plane trees up towards the small cafés.

But one sits there with an empty glass in one's hand. Tries to stop imagining the old house in Provence and Sebastian playing in the great oak trees.

Note about a House

On the plane to Nice one tries to sleep. At one's side is a woman who talks non-stop about how *wonderful* it had been on the Acropolis. The moonlight, Athens's numberless lights below one, white columns against the night sky! Back home in Fayetteville, North Carolina, neither she nor her friend Mary Lou had ever dreamed of experiencing anything like that.

One lets the woman talk. To begin with, she occasionally stops for one to say something or at least nod. One does neither. Then she stops stopping and talks the whole time while looking at or past one. If, behind closed eyes, one had considered imagining what she looked like, one wouldn't have managed it. Even if one must have seen her when one sat down.

Her words gradually fall to pieces. Her voice becomes like the steady din of the aircraft engines. Soothing, soporific. Nevertheless one doesn't sleep. When one closes one's eyes, they appear – the fantasies about the house among the oak trees in Provence. The house Bob Ridgway said one had to have seen in order to understand Sebastian.

Ever since this young man left one at the harbour, it had been like a constantly changing mist before the fishing-boats, the black-clad women, the stars beyond the window at night. Flickering, sketchlike scenes from the house in Provence that had leapt from the stories of Penelope, Camilla and Wilhelm. Sebastian as a naked Pan in the oak during afternoon tea, seducing his younger sister while his brother watches . . . charming his grandmother into serving him chocolates and wine . . . bewitching his elder, repressed sister in the darkness of the night!

One took the dog into bed with one at night. Held on to the animal body so that one didn't see the flickering scenes. Then it sometimes happened that one slept. One night, one awakened and thought one lay in Camilla's entreating arms. It was the dog's paws one had felt. Nauseated, one pushed it away. Unconcerned, it slid to the floor and disappeared into the darkness.

One didn't go back to sleep.

Through the breaks in the cloud cover, the coast of Italy can be dimly perceived. The woman interrupts herself to ask if she could have seen Vesuvius on the way to Ajaccio. Back home in Fayetteville, North Carolina, both she and her friend Mary Lou had always dreamt of getting to see Vesuvius. Was it really a fact that red-hot lava flowed from the crater sometimes?

One doesn't hear her.

One is thinking about why one is sitting there.

Sebastian, with the hairless skin and features from the pictures Penelope showed one, had become more and more insistent. But the face was nevertheless unclear, as if covered by a membrane. In order to avoid him, one tried to focus all one's attention on a detail of a boat, on a shadow, on one's pastis glass. But ever more frequently these impressions were displaced by Sebastian's indistinct, unbearably present face. One rises, walks to another room, to the harbour; to places where one had never before set foot. In vain.

One morning, one suddenly drank one's pastis to the last drop, put one's glass down on the marble table-top and walked to the little travel bureau in a harbour side-street. There, one booked a place on the first plane from Ajaccio to Nice.

Like a man pursued.

One stands at the window in a post office. On the walls hang posters with pictures of holiday destinations: Antibes, Monte Carlo, Cagnes, St Tropez, Cannes. One lets one's glance glide indifferently over sandy beaches with half-naked people, romantic castles, picturesque alleys that remind one of theatre scenery. An elderly man beyond the window searches in catalogue after catalogue for the Warden address. Provence is a big place. Has one no idea where they live? One shrugs one's shoulders. The man sighs and picks up the telephone. One again looks distantly at the posters. Hears him spell out 'Warden' distinctly. After a while asking: Beatrice Warden?

One turns as the man says: Near Aix. In a village south of Aix.

Smiling, he pushes a piece of paper with the address towards one through the window. Without looking at it, one puts it into one's pocket and goes. Doesn't see the smile that slowly disappears.

The large wrought-iron gate is securely locked. One pulls on a handle and a bell rings far away. But no one comes. One begins walking along the fence. It is drizzling, and one's shoes become wet in the grass. Why does one put up with this? In one place the fence has fallen down. One steps over it and into the Warden family's woods.

Nearer the house the landscape becomes more like a park. Unmowed lawns, overgrown gravel pathways, scattered oak trees and cypresses. A white painted table stands under an old oak. That must be where Penelope was seduced by Sebastian while Wilhelm watched, and their grandmother drank afternoon tea. One tries to see it for oneself. Sebastian as a naked Pan in the tree, and Penelope flirting obligingly. But she said nothing about Wilhelm. Didn't she see him, or wasn't he there? Was Wilhelm's account of what occurred only fantasy?

It has begun to grow dark. The house is like a ponderous stone outcrop among the trees. There are no lights anywhere, neither in the windows nor outside the doors. One sits on the edge of the table, feels a cold dampness against one's thighs.

One glances at one's watch. No one could have gone to bed so early. Perhaps no one is living in the house. Perhaps it is many years since any Warden has lived there.

Did any of them speak the truth?

One has a feeling of being observed. That Sebastian is sitting in the tree and following one with his eyes. That his grandmother is looking at one over her teacup. That Penelope is peeking teasingly at one while half-consciously she caresses her necklace.

One rises and walks towards the house. None of the outer doors can be opened. All the windows are closed. On the terrace in front of the house one stops, pulls the sleeve of one's jacket down over one's hand and smashes a pane in the french windows. The glass tinkles down on the floor inside. One stands there listening. No one has heard anything. No one is coming. One thrusts one's hand through the opening left by the smashed pane, turns the key on the inside and opens the french windows.

After finding one's way to the electric switch, one turns on the ceiling light. It is a big room with French art on the walls. A painting by Degas is the only work of real value. A group of easy chairs stand by a low, broad fireplace, another around a table at the largest window. A large grand piano, an old camphor wood chest, some straight-backed chairs along the walls and a writing-desk set at an angle in a corner given the room a restless, overloaded quality.

One stiffens. On the table by the window stands a half-full wine decanter and two glasses. One lifts one of the glasses and holds it up against the light. Is it still moist at the bottom?

Is there someone living in the house after all?

Slowly, one walks up the stairs to the first floor, stops at regular intervals and listens. Not a sound. The long corridor has many doors. One for each member of the family, one thinks. Some are closed, others stand half-open. One peers in; they seem like nurseries. For how many years have they stood so?

One opens a door. The room inside is larger than the others. It must be the grandmother's. One stands there quietly on the threshold, accustoms oneself to the light from the night beyond the window in order to see if anyone is lying in the wide bed. An old woman's head on the pillow? But the bed is empty.

Then one goes in, lights the lamp on the night table and sits down on a chair. There is a box of chocolates on the night table, and hesitantly one takes one. It is shrunken and grey-brown and has almost no taste. Has it been lying there since Sebastian's last sudden visit?

Beside the chocolate box stands a photograph of Sebastian in a silver frame. One recognizes it from one of the albums Penelope showed one. One is struck once more by his beauty and his agelessness. Like the portrait of Dorian Gray, one thinks with a vague memory of Oscar Wilde's tale of a man's unchanging appearance.

One whispers – as if the old woman is lying asleep in the wide bed after all: What kind of a person was he really? Never met him, want to have nothing to do with his fate. Won't have anything to do with anyone. The world is the harbour with the fishing-boats, the black-clad women, the table with the marble top, the glass of pastis. Unchangeably. Despite that, one is sitting here now. Can you explain it?

The face, which isn't there, turns towards one with open eyes. The thin lips move. The voice is barely audible. One must bend forward to understand what is being said.

Sebastian, this unfortunate boy, filled everyone with a light. A faith. When he suddenly entered the room – no one could guess where from – the stiffness and the pains in that old body of mine disappeared. Fetch the wine! I called. Fetch the chocolates from the cupboard! And to poor, thin Camilla, who bore them forth so radiantly, he gave beauty.

Does one hear a laugh?

One afternoon, Penelope and I were sitting at the table under the old oak out in the garden drinking tea. She was only a heedless child, and I thought: Who in the world can transform her into a woman? Sebastian! He was already sitting in the tree naked as a god of the woods. As if he was granting my prayer, he playfully glided down and loved love into her against the tree trunk. They didn't notice me. Nor they did they see their brother Wilhelm who, filled with jealousy and admiration, followed his sister's transformation from the window of his room.

That's exactly what you must remember, came the whisper from the pillow, when you write the book now about Sebastian. He was like a healer. His hands changed us. Smoothed away the distress in us, the sorrow.

But there won't be any book about Sebastian!

The face isn't there. One rises and pulls the bedclothes aside. The sheet is taut and smooth. The pillow bears no impression of any head. Then one sinks down on one's knees, leans one's forehead against the edge of the bed. Is it tears? Rage?

One grasps the picture of Sebastian and smashes the glass against the corner of the night table. The pieces fly in all directions. One tears the photograph from the silver frame. Throws the frame on the floor. Glass crunches when one walks towards the door. But with one's hand on the doorknob, one turns, stands there looking at the picture. One walks back some steps, picks it up and puts it in one's inside pocket.

On the way across the grass between the cypresses and the oak trees, one looks back just one time. The house is again like a stone outcrop against the night sky. A light is shining in a first-floor window. Didn't one put out the lamp on the night table?

One stops for a moment, walks on.

Dark Longing

The night plane to Ajaccio doesn't leave for some hours. One could have stayed till next morning, but can't bear to. Can't bear to find a hotel, can't bear the thought of one night more in a strange room.

One assumes that the restaurant is closed at night. Doesn't even check. On the way to the departure lounge one walks past a news-stand that is open, and a woman behind the counter gives one a quick, questioning glance: Newspapers, a book, chocolate? One ignores her. Wants only to be left in peace.

There are few people in the departure lounge. Some are trying to sleep on the hard plastic benches. Others are looking absent-mindedly at newspapers left among paper cups and loaded ashtrays. A child is running noisily among the tables. One thinks: At any moment that kid's going to take a tumble!

One sits down in a corner far away from the exit. The neon light is as strong there as usual in the lounge, but it doesn't matter. One tries to think of nothing. But the picture of Sebastian rises to the surface. Why did one take it with one? To restrain oneself from taking it out of one's pocket and looking at it, one thinks about the harbour with the fishing-boats. Closes one's eyes to recall the shrieking of the seagulls and the smell of fresh-caught squid. It's no use. Sebastian's ageless face is there the whole time.

As if one were an outside observer, one sees oneself take out the

picture. A middle-aged man – unshaven because he didn't get around
to bringing his shaving things – who bends forward with his elbows on
his knees and a photograph in his hands. That slender form . . . is it
felt as a kind of pain? But one sits there looking.

A shadow falls upon the photograph. A woman stands before one.
Her turned-up coat collar gives her a youthful appearance. She smiles
without smiling. Her eyes regard one calmly, as if she knows who one
is. Her voice is cool.
  My name is Claudette Brisson. I was Sebastian's psychiatrist. The
Wardens said I would find you here, and that you should talk with me.
  The Wardens?
  That's right.
  Had one been seen after all by someone or other in that apparently
deserted house? Or did they keep one under surveillance? One
doesn't inquire. It is unimportant, and besides, even if she knows
something, she will hardly answer.
  There is nothing to talk about!
  She stands there calmly, gives the impression she doesn't notice
that, without taking one's eyes from her face, one puts the photograph in one's jacket pocket. But she must have seen it.
  She says: Give me your ticket, so that I can arrange for you to take
the morning flight tomorrow. You can sleep at my place after we have
had a chat.

Claudette Brisson's flat has white walls, ceiling and furniture. Only
the carpet, some cushions and a couple of abstract paintings have
colours. One stands there in it coolly unmoved. As she throws her
coat over the back of a chair, she says: You haven't eaten since this
morning, so you must have some food. It'll only take a moment. In
the meantime, you can shave. You'll find a shaver on the shelf in the
bathroom.
  One remains standing there.
  How does she know when one last ate?

She comes from the kitchen with one plate, some meat, bread, two glasses and a bottle of wine. One hasn't moved. She sits down on a sofa, draws her legs up under her and pours wine into one of the glasses. She sips it as if it doesn't concern her that one is standing. Or as if she knows that one is going to sit down. That it is only a question of time.

At last one sits down, but not by the plate, and thinks: Why didn't one say no and take the night plane? Then one would have been home in only a few hours. Been oneself.

Drive back to the airport!

She shakes her head.

In connection with your work on the book about Sebastian, there's something you must know. His death came to his family unexpectedly. To me it was almost inevitable. . . .

One gets up so suddenly that the table overturns. Everything goes on the floor. The china and glasses are smashed, and the wine flows slowly over the carpet. One shouts that one isn't working on any book, and that one doesn't want to know anything about Sebastian. That he is someone of total unimportance!

Again she smiles without smiling.

Then why did you come here, break into the country house, steal Sebastian's picture and sit unable to take your eyes from it?

Powerless, one sinks down on the chair again. One looks at Claudette Brisson. So strange. Her skin seems quite smooth, her eyelashes longer than one remembers and her half-length hair is almost blue-black. One stretches out one's hand to touch her, but isn't able to. One feels a need to be embraced, and one's body remembers – faintly – a heavy warmth from a distant past. Of an almost forgotten woman's caress, of a son's touch. One closes one's eyes. Scarcely hears Claudette Brisson's voice:

Sebastian is the longing for death in you. That's why you are fascinated and repelled by him. I know it from myself. Many of my patients have wanted to die, but only he has been the longing for death itself. After my hours with him – after having looked into the black nothingness that was in his mind – I would sometimes lie down as if to die. Even if you are only writing about him, you must have done so, too – lain on your back with your hands on your breast as if in a sarcophagus and waited. At last the disappointment that life doesn't forsake you. It was to say this that I agreed to see you.

But one is just indescribably tired.

It is as dark as it can be in an entirely white bedroom when the light from the street filters in through the curtains. Claudette Brisson lies naked beside one and looks towards the ceiling. Her voice is cool, as if to nullify her nakedness: They say that people *en route* to obliteration lie with one another like animals. Perhaps that's why, ever since I detected the longing for death in and through Sebastian, I've constantly sought sexual intercourse as an outlet. Have you done so, too?

One hasn't had any longing for death!

Or has one? The eternal repetition, the empty house, the solitude on the island? But one was also like that before one knew about Sebastian! A car outside casts light that glides over the ceiling. One follows it with one's eyes, while one thinks about what caused one to sleep with Claudette Brisson. An act as impossible to remember as a pain, at best only as an observation from a corner in the darkness: two sweaty bodies in despairing struggle to experience, each for itself, the opposite of death. The far-off hint of warmth, of the almost forgotten woman, of the son's touch was no longer in one.

One hears her say, matter-of-factly: Actually I wasn't sleeping with you, but with Sebastian. I saw him in front of me the whole time. The ageless and young-girlish Sebastian. Felt that it was him I was embracing. Didn't you feel that, too? I'm certain that several times you even called his name.

Did one? Did one call Sebastian and see in front of oneself the form from the pictures Penelope showed one? One perceives it dimly like a dream, but can't remember whether it was Claudette Brisson's voice or one's own that one heard. Whether it was with her body or his that one saw oneself struggling.

One closes one's eyes once more in order not to see.

Not until Claudette Brisson has put on her coat, has turned up the collar and stands holding the front-door handle in the morning does one ask – almost in order to have asked – if the Wardens knew about Sebastian's longing for death. Asks about why they thought one should talk to her.

Or perhaps they didn't think that?

She shrugs her shoulders.

Then she walks out to the car. One follows her and sits down in it beside her. She drives as one might have imagined, with quick, sure movements. It doesn't take many minutes for one to reach the airport.

Neither says a word.

The cold strikes against one when one opens the door of the house behind the garden wall. One hasn't noticed that before. Nor that the rooms are like strangers. As if one doesn't live there at all, but sees them again and again for the first time.

A faint sound causes one to turn round. It is the dog that glides across the threshold. Then one kneels and lays one's cheek against its grey snout. How long does one stay like that? One strokes its body, unconsciously. Its bones almost stick out through its skin. Can it have become like that in only the day and night one was in Provence?

In a kitchen cupboard one finds the remains of a sausage, which one cuts up on a plate. Puts it on the floor. Hesitantly, the dog walks over, lies down and eats. Slowly. One has never seen any other animal eat like that.

And one believes everything is as it was.

But the picture of Sebastian lies in one's jacket pocket. It has acquired creases, which one tries to straighten out. It can't be done, and one throws it in the fireplace. One changes one's mind and props it against a vase on the table.

It stands there looking at one.

Monologue with Tears

One is awakened by the telephone, but just lets it ring. It rings so seldom that one forgets it between times. Forgets to see about getting it removed. For what does one want with a telephone?

When one has got out of bed, it rings again, but one still doesn't answer it. It is probably a wrong number, and if it actually is someone who wants to speak to one, there is even less reason for answering. After one has been down to the harbour, looked at the fishing-boats and drunk one's glass of pastis, it rings at regular intervals throughout the afternoon. It is as if the sound becomes stronger and stronger.

At last one can't bear it any more and lifts the receiver. But one doesn't say anything – just listens tensely to a man who asks several times if anyone is there. One's breathing must have betrayed one, for the man says – apparently unconcerned at not having received any answer – that he is Richard Warden, Sebastian's father, and that it is his understanding one wishes to speak to him. If it isn't too inconvenient, he continues, he will gladly come the very next day on his way to London. But if it isn't convenient, he can naturally visit one on a later occasion.

One thinks: How disarmingly polite they are, these people. As if they know that then one can't refuse them.

Obviously it's convenient!

Richard Warden is a tall, handsome man. Short hair and beard,

carefully shaved on the cheeks and around the mouth, frame his face.
If one knows that Sebastian was his son, one sees resemblances. The
long eyelashes, the slender figure, the unaffectedly self-important
glance.

After one has opened the front door, he stands there calmly until
one has expressly invited him in. Just as expressly, one must invite
him to sit down. The well-bred behaviour is like a discreet marker of
distance.

One takes out two glasses and a bottle of local wine. Slowly, like a
ritual, one places the glasses on the table and pours. Is it a counter-
move? Smilingly expressionless, Richard Warden nods, lifts his glass.
As he puts it down, he nods again. Appreciatively. His glass seems
just as full. Did he taste the wine, or was his nod only a continuance
of the ritual? A further emphasis of breeding – and distance?

Richard Warden sits there with his hand on his glass. Turns it slowly
as if studying it. But his glance is preoccupied.

There's something you should know about Sebastian's death, he
says. I'm convinced he didn't take his own life. It was what one might
call a political murder, probably carried out by a young Chinese
woman. You've already met her in Singapore, as a matter of fact –
June Wong.

One says nothing; just listens.

I don't know if you have children yourself, but you quite understand that, in our day, they live entirely their own lives. It's no longer
the case that a father guides or decides. Even advice is out of order.
When Sebastian lived with me, I knew less about him than I know
about my employees in the shipping firm. Now I reproach myself that
I didn't try to know more. That I didn't take seriously what was
hinted about him.

He raises his glass as if to drink, but puts it down on the table
again. He trembles when it is in his hand.

It was mentioned to me, though perhaps not in so many words, that
he smuggled weapons. You may think it strange, but he received a
great deal of money from me. As you know, he had his own aero-

plane, and I thought the money went on pleasure trips to Sydney, Hong Kong, Bangkok. It was the only thing I felt I could give him. Now I realize that the money was spent on weapons that were picked up and delivered in the plane. Something must have happened – maybe a conflict between rival groups of rebels – and he was killed. He looks at one helplessly. I didn't suspect what he was doing. Then one realizes that he is crying. All along, one has seen that his cheeks are moist. One has just been unaware that it is caused by tears. Not with a single glance does one betray that one sees him crying.

Actually, Richard Warden continues, neither of us knew anything about the other's life. When Sebastian was in Singapore, I used to have breakfast with him. I was his father, after all. Naturally, I heard then about all his madcap notions, and we enjoyed my small Malaysian mistresses. But we never talked together – just exchanged delightful anecdotes. He adds: Maybe that was the wrong thing? The anecdotes? One has emptied one's own glass. Richard Warden has hardly touched his. He bends forward and asks softly and apologetically if he may be permitted to pour some wine. One is bewildered by the guest offering, but nods. He takes the winebottle and pours. At the same time, the tears stream down his cheeks. Does he know that both know it, even if neither lets on that the tears are streaming?

Richard Warden waits politely. For one is drinking. What else can one do? When one has put down the glass again, he says with a voice that is still low and apologetic: Sebastian was a problem for me when he lived. Roving and indefinable. I thought: He'll never be able to take over the shipping company! He'll never become a man! Sometimes I said I didn't know him. He laughed then. Now I don't understand how I could see him like that. Now I see that he was more a man than any of us. Was himself. I don't know whom he was

backing by smuggling weapons. But he took chances – risked his life –
for people he believed in. Ideas he believed in. I didn't see that. Now
I know I should have seen it.

Then he says, in a still lower voice: You're the only person I've told
this to.

One can't forget his tears. Long after Richard Warden has gone, one
sits there seeing them in front of one. That is, sees in front of one a
man apparently unmoved by a sorrow that is forced in upon him. As
if his tears come from a source he doesn't know, perhaps can't
acknowledge face to face with another person.

One tries to imagine Richard Warden when he is alone. Is he able
then to feel his tears? Can he then cry out his despair? Does his voice
crack then?

It is impossible to tell. One is forced to stop thinking about it. To
forget his tears altogether! Then other images appear: father and son
at the breakfast table. One anecdote succeeds the other. They col-
lapse with laughter.

As if each is laughing from his own world.

It is beginning to grow dark. But one doesn't turn on the lights,
doesn't notice the dog by the fireplace. One just sits and sees them in
front of one – father and son. The picture is altered, slides over into
memory. The son becomes less and less Sebastian and is changed into
a little boy in the kitchen of a house one suddenly deserted. He grows
before one's eyes, begins to talk, ask questions, think things. Indig-
nantly: Father, why don't you do anything?

Did one make any reply?

The boy's face comes somehow towards one in the half-darkness.
Has one ever seen it so clearly? So helplessly naked? Quite unexpectedly, the tears are felt. From deep within, they fill one's eyes and
stream slowly down one's cheeks.

Why did one let Richard Warden come?

From a letter one will perhaps never complete or ever post:

You believe, perhaps, that your father has forgotten both you and those times at the breakfast table. He hasn't. Because of something that happened, which can't be more explicitly referred to, you suddenly became quite visible at home in the blue kitchen. Or was it that kitchen in one's own childhood that was blue? In any case, you were remembered, and without there being any explanation, a strange want arose. Please realize that! But you asked questions, and your opinions demanded plain action.

So please realize, too, if you don't already, that there comes a day in a person's life when one no longer knows if the need to act comes from outside or from within. If it is caused by inner conviction or fear of not living up to other people's expectations.

Who do you think one is, anyway?

The boy's face is still there. The words on the sheet of paper haven't rubbed it out. But the tears are gone. Then one notices that the dog has lifted itself up and sits watching one. That strangely penetrating look! How long has it been sitting there like that, without moving?

One kneels and takes the dog's head in one's hands. Holds it frighteningly tight. But the look doesn't waver. Then tears explode behind one's eyes again. One gets up suddenly and walks out into the garden.

The coldness of the night beats against one.

Dialogue without Words

One sits on the plane to Singapore, the city to which one doesn't want to return. But one is without any will. Something alien – some stranger – has taken up residence inside one. Or is it a power that has always been there, hidden? One has no strength to resist what is happening.

In wonder, one felt this stranger within order tickets with one's own voice, take one along with it to the airport, guide one aboard the plane. The stranger whispered: You must see June Wong again, the Chinese girl who loved Sebastian. One didn't want to, but nodded. Like a sleep-walker.

Frightened, one discovers the sea beneath one.

June Wong. Why did this stranger whisper that one must see her again? Fortunately, one has managed to forget her. One tries to recall her, but sees before one only a typical young Chinese woman. Indistinctly as a rule, now and then more clearly – as if through a camera one isn't able to focus properly. In a fleeting glimpse or two, it is almost sharp: a cool and sallow face. Is it pretty? Then it is enclosed again, as if by a mist.

The face is transformed, acquires a body. A slender, young woman's body. What is that in the background? Notre-Dame? It must be Notre-Dame in Paris, for one sees the bookstalls, the bridges, the barges along the quays, the pigeons and the men who fish so tirelessly. One sees oneself, too. Hand in hand, one walks with her from bookstall to bookstall on the quayside, hunts for old books, and she smiles at one. Radiantly! She throws her arms around one, as if the two are alone, or as if it doesn't matter that everyone can see. One becomes one with her, this pretty person. It is like a promise. A promise of a life, of an eternity!

One doesn't want to remember.

This time, too, one sleeps and hardly notices where the plane stops on the way. But when the plane is approaching Changi Airport, and people are trying to catch a glimpse of the city of Singapore, one becomes restless. The stranger inside one – the thing one still doesn't want to realize has anything to do with one – whispers: Soon you will meet June Wong.

One needn't ask anyone where one shall go. The stranger inside one whispers that, too. When one gets into the taxi, one says curtly to the driver: Tua Poh.

It is humid and hot. One's clothing sticks to one's body. One leans back in the seat and closes one's eyes. This driver, too, asks if this is one's first time in Singapore. One doesn't answer now, either.

One knows that the noise of the traffic will be succeeded by cries in a language one doesn't understand, that the street is cramped with clothes hung out to dry on poles, and that children stretch out their hands for money when the taxi stops. One knows that one won't even look at them.

The driver wants to bring one into the courtyard. But one doesn't want him to tag along. One has been there before. Chickens, pigs and half-naked youngsters all mixed up together. As on the former occasion, some old people are sitting on a flight of steps, and a younger woman is cooking food under a tin roof.

Now, too, a little girl comes with a chicken in her arms. To show it to one? A gift? One pushes her aside. The woman under the tin roof smiles cautiously. Impatiently, one asks: June Wong?

The cautiously smiling woman rises from the cooking-pot and walks towards a doorway with a ragged curtain. Her look says that one should follow her. By a narrow hallway one comes into a dark room. Gradually one makes out a television set on a box, a low table, a mattress on the floor. On the mattress sits a young woman with her legs drawn up under her.

One understands that it is June Wong.

Slowly she turns around and looks at one with vacant eyes. Does she recognize one? One sits down on the table. The mattress is too low, too near June Wong. Hesitantly, one says: June, you must tell what you know about Sebastian.

Was there a tiny movement that betrayed that she heard what one said? But she says nothing, just sits motionless. One grows uncertain. But it *is* June Wong! After getting used to the dim light, one can clearly see and recognize her features. She *is* the young Chinese woman one met in the bird sanctuary.

June, one repeats, you must tell what you know about Sebastian. You well understand what one is saying. You are also capable of answering. You spoke fluent English in Jurong, where you work.

Or didn't she do so at all? It occurs to one that she may be under the influence of something. Her slow movements and her vacant expression suggest it. One bends forward to see if the pupils of her eyes are small, as one remembers they become with those who have taken opium or morphine. But the light is so weak that her eyes are merely like empty, black shadows in her sallow face.

One observes her while one speaks.

Some think it was you who killed Sebastian. You didn't. But you yourself must say you didn't murder him. That you loved him and aren't to blame for his death.

She turns her head away. As if in dread?

Her neck muscles quiver.

One has seen it before, but doesn't want to remember! Decades ago, a woman on a bed in a half-dark room. In America? Her face averted, her neck muscles quivering. Like taut bowstrings. One shook her, cried out: What's the matter with you? Answer!

She merely sat with averted face. What was she feeling? One never got to know. Or did one repress it? But one didn't manage to forget the averted face, the quivering neck muscles. Still one tried, because in fact one felt pity – felt warmth – for another person. Fortunately, it comes to one only in momentary flashes.

One feels a hint of pity and warmth. But only a hint and one fights against it. Why feel anything for a random Chinese woman? But the rooms, the forms and the faces merge into one another. With all one's strength, one holds on to the fact that one is in Singapore. That the woman is June Wong! One takes hold of her shoulders and shakes her, cries out: What's the matter with you? Answer!

Again, one feels a hint of tears and shakes her more – shakes her ever more violently. Her head rocks passively from side to side. At last one releases one's grip on her shoulders, and one's hands slide towards the nape of her slender neck. Almost without knowing it, one holds her against oneself. In wonder, one notices that cheek touches cheek. One whispers: June, even if you had him killed. . . .

Her body gives a start, quivers tensely. But she doesn't tear herself free. One can still feel her cheek against one's own. Was it an answer? A yes, a no? Had she killed him or had him killed in spite of – or because of – the fact that she loved him?

June, why don't you say anything?

One gets a strange feeling. Are one's cheeks becoming smooth, one's hair longer – blue-black? One sees oneself as if from somewhere out in the half–dark room. Hears a voice. One's own?

June, you're right about the Wardens. They think they can get everything for money. Even a book. And they want to prevent one from fighting for the oppressed. Prevent one from talking to the poor no one will admit exist in this country – from saying they mustn't

acquire colour TV sets, but knowledge. Power. From telling how Lee
Kuan Yew exploits the weak.
One sees a hint of a smile.
What is happening? One feels her holding one, tightly, as if she will
never let go. Does she believe that one is Sebastian? Does one
believe it oneself? One tries to pull free; simply can't. But it isn't her
strength that hinders one, it is the warmth in her hands, in her cheek
against one's own. In her slender body.
She looks earnestly at one. What is it her look says? That she
unwillingly had him killed? That he was killed by the oppressed? That
he took his own life in despair? Her dark eyes, her hands holding one
convulsively, give no answer. They express only sorrow.

Even this has happened to one before. In New York? The memory
breaks willed oblivion. To be held – wordlessly, convulsively, burn-
ingly. To feel that time is suspended, that one can sit like that with
one's arms around another person for a lifetime. That one will never
be able to let go, to get free!
What kind of eyes did she have? What sorrow weighed her down?
One has forgotten all that, thank God. In a flash, it threatens to force
its way out of oblivion, but one manages to prevent it. Manages to
prevent June Wong from awakening a longing and a sympathy that
never should have been.
That must never recur.

Finally, one is able to suppress the stranger that took residence inside
one, and get out in the courtyard again. Stopped by the dazzling
sunlight, one stands there among the chickens, pigs and half-naked
youngsters. Did June Wong just lie there looking blindly after one,
when one lurched out through the narrow hallway? The old people
on the flight of steps observe one slowly and without expression. The
woman under the tin roof still smiles cautiously. Or is it her missing
front teeth that make it seem like a smile?
Out in the cramped street one forces one's way through the flock of

children standing round the taxi with outstretched hands. One sees only the half-sleeping taxi-driver, not the hands. The humidity and the heat have become unbearable. One sinks back in the seat and unconsciously touches the picture of Sebastian. It is still there! Exhausted, one manages to say: Changi Airport.

The Merciful Ones

One leans back and closes one's eyes. Tries to think about the house at the top of the hill in the village north of Ajaccio. About whether the dog is sitting by the iron gate in the darkness. But one doesn't see the dog in front of one. One sees June Wong instead. For it *was* June Wong, even if she was entirely different from what she had been that morning in the bird sanctuary.

What can have happened to her?

She didn't speak, her movements were slow, her gaze dull. As if she hadn't eyes. Was it from sorrow or anguish or opium? Had someone tried to erase her consciousness because of what happened to Sebastian?

Suddenly one bends forward: Drive to General Hospital!

A nurse at reception asks what is wrong with one. One says one isn't ill, but must speak to the head of the surgical department about something important. About something that has happened to a former patient at the hospital.

The nurse lets her glance glide over one. The expression in her dark eyes changes almost imperceptibly. To something between curiosity and unease?

The head surgeon is engaged.

One says that one will wait.

One sits down on a vacant chair by the wall. An old man in the chair at one's side looks up and seems about to say something. To ask what is the matter, to talk about his own illnesses. One turns away. On the other side sits a woman with a child. The child's face is covered with running sores.

One closes one's eyes.

After perhaps an hour, someone stops in front of one. One opens one's eyes again and sees a man in a green surgical gown.

I'm Dr Li Ziyang. You wanted me?

One rises.

It's about a former patient.

The doctor also lets his glance glide over one. But his eyes express neither curiosity nor unease. They are merely cool.

As you possibly realize, he says, we doctors are bound to professional silence. For that reason, I can't discuss patients with you. Neither former nor current ones. You have no right to any information except from the patient himself. Besides, you see, I'm sure, all the people who are sitting here waiting for me. Many of them from the morning onwards.

One looks straight at him.

It concerns an organ transplant that was carried out at this hospital. The patient can't give me any information. She's dead. The idea was that you might be interested.

Li Ziyang's face is still. Then he says: Come with me.

The office is a simple one. An examination couch, a light-box for X-ray pictures, an armchair behind and a spindleback chair beside the desk. One sits down on the spindleback.

Li Ziyang absently picks up a hammer for testing reflexes.

What is it you really want?

It's about a British woman, probably in her late thirties, Rose Mayfield, who suffered from atrophy of the heart muscles. Were you the one who performed her heart transplant?

How did she die?

She took her own life.

Li Ziyang puts aside the reflex hammer.

I remember well that she was depressive.

Depression, one explains, wasn't the cause. The heart was taken from a young man, Sebastian Warden, immediately after he had committed suicide. She felt that the dead man had started living inside her. That he had been resurrected against his will. So she had to repeat his suicide.

One thinks: Will he believe this story?

It appears so. Li Ziyang again picks up the reflex hammer and strikes it lightly a few times against the palm of his left hand. Then he takes a folder from a drawer in the desk and slowly leafs through the papers inside. Asks: How do you know who the donor was?

Rose Mayfield said so. She found it out by asking for all the newspapers – said she wanted to see if there was anything about the transplant in them. That sounded reasonable, for at the time a heart transplant was an event. But what she wanted was to find out if there was someone you could have got the heart from. In one of the papers she found the picture of a very handsome man who had shot himself. She also remembered that those who brought the heart to the operating-theatre were surprised that such a handsome man had committed suicide.

But she was anaesthetized!

That's just what she said herself. That she was like a consciousness at large in the room, and that she saw the operation from there. She described in detail how you divided her breastbone, bent it apart with a retractor and removed the diseased heart before you inserted Sebastian Warden's. That was when she heard the surprised comment about such a handsome man taking his own life.

Li Ziyang looks expressionlessly towards the window and says as if to himself that there is much one doesn't know about human consciousness.

One continues: Perhaps she committed suicide without reason.

Li Ziyang turns slowly towards one.

What do you mean?

That possibly Sebastian Warden didn't take his own life, but was

killed. As you'll remember, I'm sure, several circumstances suggested
that. But they didn't find any motive. There was no one, for instance,
who thought that it was the need of a heart.

Li Ziyang is calm, smiling.

Do you think that my colleagues and I would have killed this
Sebastian Warden to obtain a new heart for a quite random, middle-
aged British woman? Then I must be permitted to remind you that a
doctor's duty is to save, not take, life.

One returns his smile.

Actually one wasn't thinking of the British woman, Dr Li Ziyang.
One was thinking of you. According to what one understands, you
were one of the first in South East Asia to carry out a successful heart
transplant. So the thought is not unreasonable that you may have
gone to considerable lengths to work on in such an important field.
You may also have known about Sebastian Warden's difficult life and
thought that you could spare him that.

Li Ziyang is still smiling. He looks at one considerately, as if one is a
patient who fantasizes before an operation that threatens his life.

How would we have committed the murder, then?

One points out that naturally neither Li Ziyang nor his colleagues
would have carried it out themselves. For a suitable sum of money,
they would have got his girl-friend, June Wong – or Wong June, as
they probably call her – to commit it. That when one saw her a few
hours ago, something had happened. She seemed deadened. As if by
drugs.

Li Ziyang's face grows serious.

That is a tragedy which unfortunately strikes many young people in
this country. After her friend died, it has undoubtedly been a way to
meet her sorrow.

But she wasn't like that the first time, at the bird sanctuary. She
was a strong and lively woman then. Now she's without consciousness. As if someone wanted to prevent her from revealing something.

Again Li Ziyang smiles cautiously.

When you write your book about Sebastian Warden, I think you should be careful about letting the author in you gain the upper hand and distort the factual circumstances of his life. Nevertheless I shall continue your flight of fancy. Because it interests me. Purely in principle. Who's told you about the book?

If – I say *if* expressly – my colleagues and I had wished to obtain a heart for the transplant, there are clearly simpler ways than taking the life of a well-known foreign shipowner's son. Almost every day we take in people who've been the victims of accidents or violence. Many of them have no relatives who accompany them. It's an easy matter to let death become a natural exit.

One is hardly listening. One asks oneself if this man knows more than he appears to. Was that bit about the book a slip of the tongue?

If – and again I say *if* – we had procured hearts in this way, would it have been immoral? We would have gained experience and could have saved far more valuable lives than those that were lost a trifle too early. The British woman is perhaps an unfortunate example because she took her own life. But as a source of knowledge, the transplant was invaluable.

If – and once more I say *if* – we had had Sebastian Warden killed, would it have been ethically indefensible? He was a menace both to himself and to others. A rebel for rebellion's sake. Perhaps his heart was his only contribution to his fellow-men. You must detach this from your feelings for a person you haven't even met, and see it as an expression of mercy – towards himself, towards those nearest to him and towards those who have their lives prolonged.

One rises slowly. Stands there looking at Dr Li Ziyang. Looking at his smooth face, his cool eyes, his faint smile. His slender hands toy with the reflex hammer. Was he deft with the scalpel?

The taxi has its engine running. One leans back in the seat. What made the doctor think that one feels anything for Sebastian? Didn't he understand that Sebastian doesn't concern one? That *no one* concerns one?

For a moment, one feels a burning heat in one's cheeks – that one is somehow holding someone in the darkness. Holding June Wong? One straightens up suddenly and meets the driver's questioning look in the mirror. Says again, exhausted: Changi Airport.

Note about a Fraud

The dog isn't at the gate. One enters the house. Tries not to think about it. The rooms, which are like cells, seem still more barren than one remembers. Naked, empty. One catches oneself looking for the dog in room after room, although one knows it couldn't have got in. Listens for the sound of its claws on the stone floor. Suddenly one thinks one sees it lying by the fireplace. It is only a shadow. Perhaps not even that.

What has one to do in this house?

From something that is perhaps a letter one must have begun on the same night, but will hardly complete:

. . . for by a strange accident that doesn't permit explanation, people have come into one's life whom it is impossible to get out of one's thoughts in spite of the fact they don't concern one, and one of them is a man whom one has never even seen, because he was murdered or committed suicide, who is always surfacing in one's consciousness. Not only does one see him in front of one, but once in Singapore one had a feeling of *being* him, and that wasn't the reason of course one came to this remote Corsican village, but in Singapore there was also a young Chinese woman in a half-dark room who was deadened by drugs because perhaps she had committed a murder, and one tried to shake life into her, but her head just dangled from side to side, and she sank suddenly against one,

97

and unconsciously one put one's arms around her and was overwhelmed by a longing – for you in Kensington Park and the trips up
the Thames and the children whose ages one doesn't know, because one can't visualize them any more at all. . . .

One looks towards the darkness outside the window. Why hasn't the
dog come? At least it usually does so when one returns after a
journey. The dog, one thinks, must have a name. Someone must
once have called it something or other. Though maybe it has never
belonged to anyone.

Before now? one thinks.

One gets up and goes out. Stands there on the doorstep and looks
into the shadows beneath the trees. But it isn't there. A feeling comes
over one, takes hold of one's breast: Something has happened to it!
One is certain something has happened. One gets a jacket and runs
down the hill towards the harbour. Forgets to lock the door. Doesn't
even close the gate.

In a flash, one sees it before one, crouching under a tree, by a wall,
behind a box. But behind which box, by which wall, under which
tree? One mustn't think, just run where one thing or another unconsciously leads one.

Down at the harbour one finds it lying against a stone wall. In the
faint light from the lamps along the pier, one sees bloody wounds in
its head and on the side of its body. Not far away stand some teenage
boys. They have stones in their hands and sneer when they catch sight
of one.

One roars at them.

They make way uneasily, but go on sneering. One of them takes a
few steps forward and throws one more stone at the dog. It hits it on
its thigh, and the dog gives a start, but remains lying. One grabs a
boat-hook that is lying on the pier and moves towards the teenage
boys. At the same moment, they vanish in the darkness.

The dog looks at one. Its eyes are dull, almost lifeless. As one kneels at its side, it slowly lifts its head and licks one's hand. But it doesn't try to get up. An uncontrollable hatred surges up in one. A hatred that makes the tears flow, and one cries out in the darkness, without words. A rage one has never felt before is almost bursting one apart. A rage against violence and injustice. In a world like ours, why hasn't one felt it before? Was it such feelings that drove Sebastian in his fight against oppression which June Wong told one about?

While the tears flow, one lifts the dog carefully, carries it up the steep hill towards the house. As one has seen in pictures people carrying wounded children in Lebanon, in El Salvador, in Eritrea. Seen and leafed on in the newspaper. Hasn't wanted to see! Now one feels the slack body of the animal in one's arms and the blood from the wounds pressing through one's shirt. One sees a child's, a woman's, an old man's face resting against one's upper arm, distorted with pain. One closes one's eyes to shut these visions out. When one opens them again one sees the dog. Its dark muzzle hangs down. Its eyes are without focus. A horrible thought: Is the dog dead?

Why hasn't it got a name?

Up to now, its namelessness has been unimportant. Names describe, bind, create relationships. Namelessness was an advantage. But not now. One wished so fervently one could have whispered a name.

One pushes the door open with one's elbow. Inside the house, one snatches the bedspread from the bed and puts it on the floor in front of the fireplace. Carefully, one lays the dog down. When one gets up again, it follows one with its eyes. What do they express? Anxiety that one will leave it?

One kneels and puts one's arms round its neck. Has one done that to a person? One feels its moist tongue against one's cheek. One thinks again: Why haven't you got a name?

One hears oneself whisper: You mustn't disappear!

Where do the words come from? An image surfaces. One stands with one hand on the doorknob; in the other one has a suitcase. A woman is lying on the bed, whispering that she mustn't lose one, that one mustn't disappear.

But one must!

The face one has known for half one's life one no longer knows. It doesn't concern one. It is alien, like everything else. So one closes the door and leaves. Only now, kneeling by the dog, does one see the face again. Its features appear, more clearly than then.

One straightens up to examine its wounds. They are bleeding no longer, don't seem deep. They should be cleaned. With what? One doesn't have anything in the house. One could ask the people next door, but one doesn't even know what they look like. Cautiously, one lets one's hand glide over the dog to feel if anything is broken. One presses lightly on its shoulders, chest and hips. Takes its legs and moves their joints, one by one. It resists, but doesn't whine. Just raises its head as if to see what one is doing.

It's all right, one whispers. Everything's quite all right. You must just lie here quietly. There'll be a fire on in the fireplace, so you won't freeze, and you'll have food and water. Everything's all right!

After the fire has begun to burn in the fireplace, one goes out to the kitchen to get something the animal can eat. But one doesn't have anything. One runs from the house and down the hill. There must be a butcher somewhere. One finds him, forces one's way between the black-clad women up to the counter and asks for meat for a sick dog.

Doesn't see the glances around one.

One walks up the hill with the meat wrapped in a newspaper under one's arm. Slowly, breathing heavily. In the house, one goes out to the kitchen. One cuts the meat into pieces in one bowl and fills another with water. Takes the bowls in to the dog.

It isn't there!

One can't understand it. Was the front door ajar? One can't remember. But the dog could barely lift its head and look at one! Has it hidden itself, the way one has heard that dying animals do? One searches the entire house – under beds and in dark corners. In vain.

You mustn't die now!

The words are repeated like an incantation. One sinks down at the oak table. Looks at the bowls of meat and water. They are unreal, meaningless. Like toys left by a dead child. What does one do with such toys? Save them, throw them out, give them away? What did they do with what Sebastian left behind? Did they keep it as relics?

One is overwhelmed by an unexpected, desperate rage over Sebastian's death. As if he had been close to one. At the same time, a voice whispers within one: He is no concern of yours! Over the entire earth people die, are tortured, sacrifice themselves for the sake of their convictions. Every day. Shall one let oneself be crushed by their pain? Besides, was Sebastian a victim at all?

Did he actually have any convictions?

One rises suddenly and carries the bowls out to the kitchen. Throws the pieces of meat into the bin, empties the water into the sink. One's movements are firm, mechanical.

The fire still burns in the fireplace. It is cool; one puts on more wood. Tired, one leans back in the chair by the window. Half asleep, floating between memory and dream, one sees before one Sebastian's smooth face, Richard Warden's tears, the look in June Wong's eyes. It doesn't affect one. The people have become strangers – just glide into the darkness and disappear.

At last the house gives one peace.

One hears scraping sounds. Steps? Reluctantly, one opens one's eyes. It is the dog. Did one forget to check if the front door is closed? It walks stiffly. Because of pain? One doesn't stretch out one's hands, doesn't kneel. Merely thinks: Why is that animal alive?

As if Death has defrauded one.

Dialogue with Wine

One is awakened by the dog standing by the bed in the half-darkness, looking at one. It doesn't utter a sound. It just looks. Nevertheless one awakens.

The wounds aren't bloody any more. Blue-black scabs have formed. But that isn't what one notices. It is the eyes. Narrow and dark with long lashes. Can an animal have such eyes? They remind one of something. One tries to remember what.

Suddenly one gets up and walks out into the living-room. The dog follows one soundlessly. One searches among books and papers on the oak table. At last one finds the picture of Sebastian.

That's where one has seen the eyes before.

One sits on one's haunches in front of the dog. Holds its dark head with both hands. It puts up with it, its eyes don't waver. They have no whites, but their form, the colour of their irises are the same. The lashes are alike. How can it have Sebastian's eyes? *Can* it have Sebastian's eyes? One knows that it is impossible. Even Sebastian can't rise again in an animal's form. But one is uneasy. The dog has become another. Something close and at the same time a stranger.

Slowly, it stretches forth its muzzle. One feels it against one's throat. Soft and hot. The Chinese girl June Wong surfaces in one's consciousness. Her cheek against one's own. That, too, soft and hot, almost burning. What is it that is happening? Conflicting feelings

103

succeed each other, memories break into the now. Thought is no longer concerned only with when one shall get up and if the weather is good enough for one to stroll down to the pavement café at the harbour for a small glass of pastis and water before walking home for a rest.

The moment isn't all-important any more.

One sits in the plane to Nice. In the morning one rang Beatrice Warden, Sebastian's grandmother, and said that one had to talk to her. The picture of Sebastian lay before one while one rang. Again and again one looked at the eyes. One didn't understand why it became more and more difficult to distinguished them from the dog's. They were an animal's, a child's. They looked at one calmly. Directly, openly.

Were they asking for something?

In the plane one takes out the picture of Sebastian. Once again. One says to oneself: Those are the dog's eyes! One knows that isn't true. To the old grandmother, one hears oneself say: Perhaps you know that one is writing a book about your grandson Sebastian. It's said that he was very close to you; therefore, it's important to talk to you about his childhood.

That isn't true either.

The large wrought-iron gate is now securely locked. As on the former occasion, one pulls on a handle and a bell rings far away. After a while, a man comes walking through the park-like garden.

An old gardener, a servant?

He unlocks the gate, lets one in. One follows him up overgrown gravel walks. The lawn is still not cut. The grass lies flat as a field after a storm. The white garden table under the oak, where Penelope was seduced by Sebastian, needs paint.

Even in daylight the house seems like a stone outcrop among the trees. Perhaps not so ponderous as one remembers. The french windows – a pane of which one broke to get inside – stand open and bang in the wind. As if the house is deserted now, too. Though was it deserted that evening?

One walks towards the french windows. Without turning, the old man continues along the short side of the house and disappears. Should one have followed him to a main entrance? One hesitates before one knocks on the frame and enters the room.

The curtains are partially drawn. Because of the furniture? One must accustom oneself to the weak light. Unconsciously, one's glance seeks the painting by Degas, the only one of real value. Beatrice Warden is sitting in one of the easy chairs by the hearth, reading. Doesn't rise. Doesn't look up, but nods as if to indicate that she knows that one has arrived.

You are welcome to sit down.

One sits down directly opposite her. Tries to see what she is reading. The slender hands conceal the title and the author's name on the cover. Her resemblance to Sebastian is striking.

How beautiful she must have been!

When will you give me the picture back?

Her voice is without reproach. She asks as if one has politely borrowed it. One remembers how one threw the silver frame on her bedroom floor. That glass crunched under foot when one left. She gives the impression of not noticing that one fails to answer.

Beatrice Warden has put the book down and looks at one. Not inquisitively, not unpleasantly, but in a soberly appraising manner. As if one had come, one thinks, to ask for a daughter's hand. Her face discloses nothing. After a while she makes an apologetic movement of her hand.

I should have served you tea, but my granddaughter is never present when one needs her. However, there's a decanter, glasses and a box of chocolates in the cupboard over there. If you will be so kind. . . .

One rises and walks to the cupboard. One remembers Camilla

obeying when Sebastian suddenly came on a visit. That the old grandmother cried: Fetch the wine! Bring the chocolates here! In imagination, one sees Camilla when she spoke about these visits. The low voice: No one paid any attention to me. But I stayed in there with them. At a distance!

One thinks: Is she here now, too?

Beatrice Warden sits with her hands in her lap until one has poured the wine. Then she raises her glass with apparent slowness. As if she is drinking from politeness. But she empties the glass, and one pours again. The chocolates disappear one by one. She takes them without looking at the box. As if she doesn't notice what she is doing. One thinks: Has she forgotten why one is here? Does she think that this is a casual morning visit? One grows uncertain, restless. Hesitates to remind her why one has come.

Once again one pours out wine.

She lifts her glass.

Don't you think it's a splendid wine? I drink little myself, but feel one must have something in the house for special occasions. My grandson Sebastian appreciated a glass when he came to visit me once in a while. He doesn't do that any more. He shot himself. It must have been in Singapore. Can you understand why? Such a thing never leads to anything but unpleasantness. Though maybe it was just as well. What else should he have done? Won't you have more wine?

One drinks cautiously.

You mentioned that you're working on a book about him. If I could only understand why! Does one have so little to write about? Sebastian had charm, seduced his sister, entertained his old grandmother in the most enchanting fashion by telling her about the distress in the world. But he *was* nothing at all. Will you be so kind as to pour a few drops more?

One does the pouring.

He didn't take any examinations, he wouldn't go into the shipping firm. He didn't even develop physically. The only thing he did was to save what he called suffering people. When you're as old as I am, you'll understand that one has to fend for oneself. If not, you'll kill yourself, too. He talked about starvation, destitution and war as if they were disasters. He didn't understand that nature brings about evolution and balance like that. The lions kill the weak members of the gnu herd. When a young animal isn't capable of surviving, it's abandoned. That doesn't happen from wickedness, but for the sake of evolution. Balance.

Beatrice Warden empties her glass, sinks back. Her chin drops. Her look isn't fixed. Is she asleep? With open eyes? Is it an attack of unconsciousness? One becomes still more uneasy. She mustn't die now! One turns towards the french windows as if to assure oneself that one can get out.

One hears her say: Sebastian brought shame on us with his suicide! Still greater than he did when he was alive. Police, journalists. Nevertheless it was a worthy action. His only one. Dominion over his own life. If he had been murdered, there wouldn't even have been that to remember.

Writing a book about him!

One tries to say something and defend to this old woman the importance of erecting a memorial to a person who with his sacrifice and effort on behalf of the weak and destitute and exploited was a living model. . . .

One has got up. Moves one's hand to one's face. As if to feel that one is the person one is. Has one used words that aren't one's own? Said that one is doing something one has never wanted to do? One looks at the woman in the easy chair. She puts down the glass she once again has emptied. If one has said anything, she has hardly understood it.

Beatrice Warden looks up. Smiling graciously: Did you want to know anything about Sebastian?

At the same time she makes a gesture towards the glass she has drained. One doesn't touch the wine decanter. Instead, one takes the picture of Sebastian out of one's pocket and tears it to pieces. Doesn't want to see the eyes any more. Throws the pieces in the hearth. She barely notices it.

Beatrice Warden is still smiling.

You should meet my grandson Sebastian. He's an unusual person. Affectionate, cheerful. The hours fade away when he's here on a visit. Even Camilla, my granddaughter, stands there in a corner listening . . . blushing a tiny bit.

Perhaps another time?

Dialogue about a Dream

One is down at the harbour early. The fishermen haven't come in yet with the morning's catch. The black-clad women are standing on the quay waiting to make their purchases. One raises one's glass of pastis and drinks. The fifth, the sixth? One doesn't even cloud it with water.

The sight of the boats, of the boxes of squid and of the women focus one on the moment. Sebastian has again and again forced his way into one's sleep with his demands. When the dog has looked at one, it has been with Sebastian's eyes.

At the harbour, one gets peace.

A blessed emptiness rises up in one. No past, no future, just fishing-boats approaching and the mild breeze from the sea.

A woman comes walking in the distance. She isn't black-clad like the other women. But it is the fact that she is strikingly commonplace that makes one notice her. Has one seen her before? A sallow face, a slender body. Absently, one thinks: Only an English woman can look like that.

It is Rose Mayfield, the woman who received Sebastian's heart. Good lord, what does she want? One quickly drinks the rest of the pastis, gets up and goes. She follows. One hears her steps behind one as one walks up the hill towards the house. She gasps for breath. Isn't her heart functioning as well as they thought it would?

Between breaths she manages to say: I shall never read your book about Sebastian!

109

One stops and turns. She sways and is going to fall. One doesn't stretch out a hand. Her eyes hunt for a place to sit. Unwillingly, one nods towards a café.

You can rest in there.

One doesn't want to go with her, but she grasps one by the arm. One accompanies her in and gets her seated at a table. One remains standing oneself. She begins searching for something in her pocket, in vain.

Can you buy some cigarettes for me?

One goes over to the proprietor, takes a packet and flings some coins on the counter. She has let her coat slip down from her shoulders and loosened her belt, as one remembers she did at the kitchen table that evening in the house. She tears open the packet, takes out a cigarette and puts it between her lips. Again she searches in vain in her coat pocket. For a match, this time? One waits a bit before one lights the cigarette for her.

As you know, she says, I shouldn't smoke. But I can't always be thinking about the heart. Can I now?

You don't wish to read about Sebastian?

She looks at the cigarette-smoke that rises, blue-white, and spreads itself beneath the ceiling. One doesn't want to be responsible for her. That is why one speaks with some formality. That is why one doesn't sit down.

She still looks at the cigarette-smoke.

You didn't like me coming. You want to sit down there at the harbour as if nothing else existed. But I had to come.

She turns towards one.

I said that Sebastian and I conceived each other. That wasn't true. Sebastian is dead. One of his muscles keeps me alive. That's all. I also said that Sebastian gave birth to my guiltlessness. But the only thing he gave birth to was a dream.

Slowly, one sits down.

About what?

She looks again at the smoke that spreads itself beneath the ceiling. Doesn't notice that the cigarette-ash has grown long and is about to fall off. Without taking one's eyes from her, one pushes an ashtray under the cigarette. The ash falls.

Maybe, she says, and follows the smoke with her eyes, it was a dream about creating a new reality for oneself. About being able to become someone other than the person one is? I don't know. But I know that one day I managed not to look at the picture any longer.

Of Sebastian?

I tore it to pieces.

But you'd never seen such a handsome person before! You lay looking at it the whole night you got it from June Wong. Realized that Sebastian was the only one you'd loved. A power radiated from the naked figure in the picture over into your hands. You said that. Didn't you?

One hears one's own voice. Trembling. Does one feel oneself betrayed? One finds one's hand approaching one's jacket pocket. To feel if one still has it, the picture one took from the bedroom of the house in Provence? Doesn't understand why one doesn't get up and go. Remains seated.

Rose, you gave each other new life!

Neither of us suspected the other's existence. The doctors gave me life. No, prolonged my life. As if it were worth prolonging.

She turns towards one.

Poor Michael! The man I was married to before Sebastian's heart turned him into a stranger. He stood by my bed and didn't understand that I could lie there studying him feature by feature without recognizing him. Without realizing that I'd been able to live with him. That I said: You must leave. I don't know you!

When the picture of Sebastian didn't exist any more, I saw Michael in front of me. Like an animal face to face with an inescapable death without suspecting what death is. I saw it by the bed that time, too. But his confused, paralysing dread didn't affect me. In memory, it did. Like a pain.

At last, I went to him. He said: I don't know you.

She takes a fresh cigarette from the packet, her fingers groping. One thinks: She hasn't told this to anyone else. It hasn't become a story yet. One closes one's eyes. As if to avoid having heard? One leans forward to give her a light. But she puts the cigarette back and pulls her coat up over her shoulders. Slowly.

Rose, don't go!

It bursts out of one. Why? One doesn't want her to stay. Doesn't want to sit opposite this sallow woman. Doesn't want to be subjected to the demanding emptiness. To a broken dream. Nevertheless it bursts out of one: Rose, don't go!

She looks at one, without expression.

I haven't anything else to say.

But Sebastian . . .?

She moves with difficulty. Each step seems to demand all she can give. The man behind the counter hurries over and opens the door for her. Ought one to have done that? She doesn't nod. One sits there watching her disappear.

One walks up the hill towards the house. Impatiently, without understanding why. Feels only an unease. Feels strangely relieved at seeing the dog lying in the shadow under a tree inside the gate. Kneels and stretches one's hand out to stroke its dark head. To feel its hot muzzle against one's throat. But it glides out of reach. One follows. It draws still farther away.

One tries to catch its evasive glance. Tries to see Sebastian's eyes in the animal's eyes. The way one thought one saw them after the dog had been stoned. Was it imagination?

At last the dog lies in a corner of the garden wall. Watches one's movements. There, one manages to throw one's arms round it. One feels its hot muzzle against one's face. Again the Chinese girl June Wong surfaces in one's consciousness. Her cheek against one's own in the half-dark room in Singapore. Almost burning.

But only a moment.

The dog twists itself loose and disappears. One doesn't see what becomes of it. One rises slowly and goes in. Doesn't look at the place in front of the fireplace where the dog has usually lain.

From one more letter one perhaps will never finish or ever send:

You probably think it strange, possibly even intrusive, to hear from one who of course is still your husband and who nevertheless has been away so long without uttering a sound. Lately, however, one's thoughts have begun to circle around the past. Those early years. Not primarily around the marriage and the child – both of which are of course not without importance either – but around the work. Around the work in society one tried to accomplish, each in one's own way and yet together. As two inseparable, unlike people.

You didn't say anything when you were deserted, but you understood well enough, perhaps, that life was without meaning for him who left you because not a person, in the end, concerned him. That the expectation that he would be delighted with his son's success, be enchanted by the grandchildren and mourn the decline and death of old friends became unbearable. That he disappeared into himself more and more frequently when the grandchildren crawled on to his lap, or when one friend or other began yet again, as if confidentially, to speak about his increasing dizziness, his cataract or his possible stomach cancer.

Then one merely thought: The world has become unimportant to one!

One's only feeling is powerlessness!

But now something has happened that can't be explained. A complete stranger took his life, an ownerless dog one doesn't even know the name of. . . .

It is night. One lies without sleeping. Is kept awake by sounds that don't exist: steps across the floor, regular breathing.

A longing that awakens unease.

Note about a Departure

There is no dawn. Morning suddenly fills the room. Blindingly. Penetrates one's body like a pain. One turns to the wall. Tries to capture a darkness, but the light won't be shut out. It explodes in every fibre.

But one doesn't get up.

One's muscles can't even bear their own weight. As if one has toppled over from exhaustion. But that isn't why one lies there. It is because the moment is no longer all-important, the eternally peaceful shelter. In the course of the night it has been compressed into a mere passageway to new, agonizing moments. Agonizing because one can't guess what they will bring.

One thinks, has been thinking the whole night: Why did Sebastian enter one's mind?

How can a man who doesn't exist – whom one has never met, who was maybe this, maybe that – make stronger and stronger demands? Demand feelings, memories, actions? Interfere with one's being and evoke a self one doesn't want to be?

A self one thinks one isn't?

One also thinks about the fishing-boats that come with the morning's catch of squid, and about the black-clad women who have been on the pier and made their purchases. As they do every single day. About the trip down to the harbour to have a small glass of pastis and water before walking home for a rest.

115

But the thought gives one no peace. It fills one with despair. One doesn't know if one can bear to see them any longer – the fishing-boats and the black-clad women. One doesn't know if one can bear any longer the taste of pastis and water.

One hears a sound. Steps? Is it the dog? One feels one's chest contract. When did that last happen? Or is it *you*? The son or the wife one left?

One catches oneself thinking: A 'you' demands an 'I'.

Someone is knocking cautiously. One almost doesn't hear it. One turns slowly. Opens one's eyes towards the light, towards the door.

Towards Penelope Warden.

The slender form in white leans against the door-frame. Faintly smiling? Calmly, she strokes her long, black hair back over her shoulders as if to let one see her face better. Recognize her.

Did I wake you up?

One doesn't answer.

May I make a little coffee for us?

She closes the door carefully. So that one will get dressed? One finds one's clothes. A piece here, a piece there. One dresses slowly. Like a prisoner on his way to the scaffold, one thinks. Why did she come? Does she think the commission is completed? That the manuscript of the book about Sebastian lies organized beside the word processor?

She has washed a pair of cups and laid the kitchen table. She has found bread and cheese. Did one have that? A coffee kettle stands on one of the gas jets. Everything seems strange. As if one hasn't been in that kitchen before.

One stands there. Says: Do you believe the commission is completed? That the manuscript of the book about Sebastian lies in a well-ordered pile beside the word processor? Well, it doesn't.

She gets the coffee kettle and pours.

I took what little I found in the cupboard.

One sits down hesitantly. On guard, like one afraid to be caught in a trap. The collar on her white pullover slips down, and one sees the necklace. It is as dented, twisted and bent as it was the first time one saw it. One feels a relief. Something to fall back on at last.

Give that to me. It must be repaired!

She touches it, smiling faintly.

No. It must stay like this. The way it usually is. The time you straightened out the dents and polished away the scratches, it became something strange. Now it isn't any more. Now it's me again.

She drinks carefully. The coffee is hot.

Why did you come anyway?

She places her cup on the table. Sits there looking at one. Searches for words? Then she raises her eyes to one.

You mustn't write about Sebastian.

One turns suddenly.

I've erased my copies of the funeral videos, she continues, and I've burned the pictures of him. You will, of course, have your expenses covered for all your preliminary work.

But you loved him, Penelope!

We all did.

One catches oneself staring at her.

Do you remember what you said about Sebastian? He was a rare person. An example to others. One who fought for the weak and oppressed in society. One who had to be honoured with a memorial for that reason – with a book you came here and absolutely begged to have written. Didn't you?

But you made us remember Sebastian as he really was. A human being like the rest of us. You talked to us. Then we began to see him – and ourselves – with your eyes. How senseless it would have been, having a book about him.

'*Your* eyes'. What had one really seen?

She gets up. All the while smiling faintly. Why does she smile? She glances at her wrist-watch, and one thinks: Commission carried out! Unfortunately I must catch the plane to Paris.

One doesn't say anything.

I hired a car at the airport. It's pleasant, but when one doesn't know one's way about, it's difficult to estimate the time.

Didn't she say that last time, too?

Now, as then, one looks at her to find out what kind of woman she is. Again, it strikes one that she is used to that. Her eyes observe one calmly while one tries to let one's glance penetrate her expressionlessness.

She takes one's hand.

I hope I didn't come at an awkward time.

The rooms feel barren as cells. The windows have no bars, but nevertheless seem as if they have. One checks that the door is unlocked, but knows that it is open. The place feels forced on one by powers one doesn't control.

Doesn't even know.

One takes one's suitcase from under the bed. Covered with dust. Throws down the few books and clothes one brought with one. One goes out to the kitchen. Casts only a glance at the cups and coffee kettle. Takes the bread, the cheese and left-overs from the refrigerator and puts them in a dish that one places outside in the shadow of a tree.

One thinks: Some dog or other will find it.

One sees it in one's imagination. Indistinctly, vaguely. The thin body that merged into the garden wall. That one first saw when the dog rose without a sound. That jumped away when one came too near, but was sitting there again next day.

Did it go with one into the house?

On the way to the airport, one drives along the harbour. The fishing-boats, the black-clad women, the table at which one usually sat. Did one drink pastis? Everything is as far away as the house one left.

At the airport one must wait.

The departure lounge is full of people, including some from one's own part of the world. One catches oneself looking at the varied faces. Expressions of sorrow, expectation, bitterness, joy. Looks, as if all of this is something one didn't know existed. One notes that some emerge from the crowd, smile searchingly and mention something one once wrote.

One nods uneasily.

Do they remember what one has almost forgotten oneself?

A young couple approach with a child they want one to smile at, perhaps say something to. Embarrassed, one tries to ask the child if it likes travelling. What else can one do? The child doesn't answer. Just stands there, looking and looking.

What have the young couple said about one?

One walks over to the news-stand. The woman behind the counter gives one a quick, questioning glance: Newspapers, a book, chocolate? One catches oneself smiling at her willingness to please. As if one usually buys things from her. Says one only wants a ballpoint and a picture postcard. She takes out some pens, shows one the selection of postcards with pictures of the harbour, an olive grove, the old fortress, fishing-boats in the grey morning light.

The picture doesn't matter.

Finds a place at a table. Pushes half-filled glasses and dirty cups aside. Sits there with the card in front of oneself and the ballpoint in one's hand. For the first time in – how long? – one's mind is bewilderingly filled with words. Words that want to say something, to bite into the moment, to lead to action. They press forward, push themselves past each other.

Like the travellers at the airport.

One word forces itself past all others from the innermost room of consciousness, frightening in its nearness. Like a person who once was everything to one, but whom one doesn't dare remember for that very reason. One bends forward over the table and tensely begins to write:

I . . .

DATE DUE

Demco, Inc. 38-293

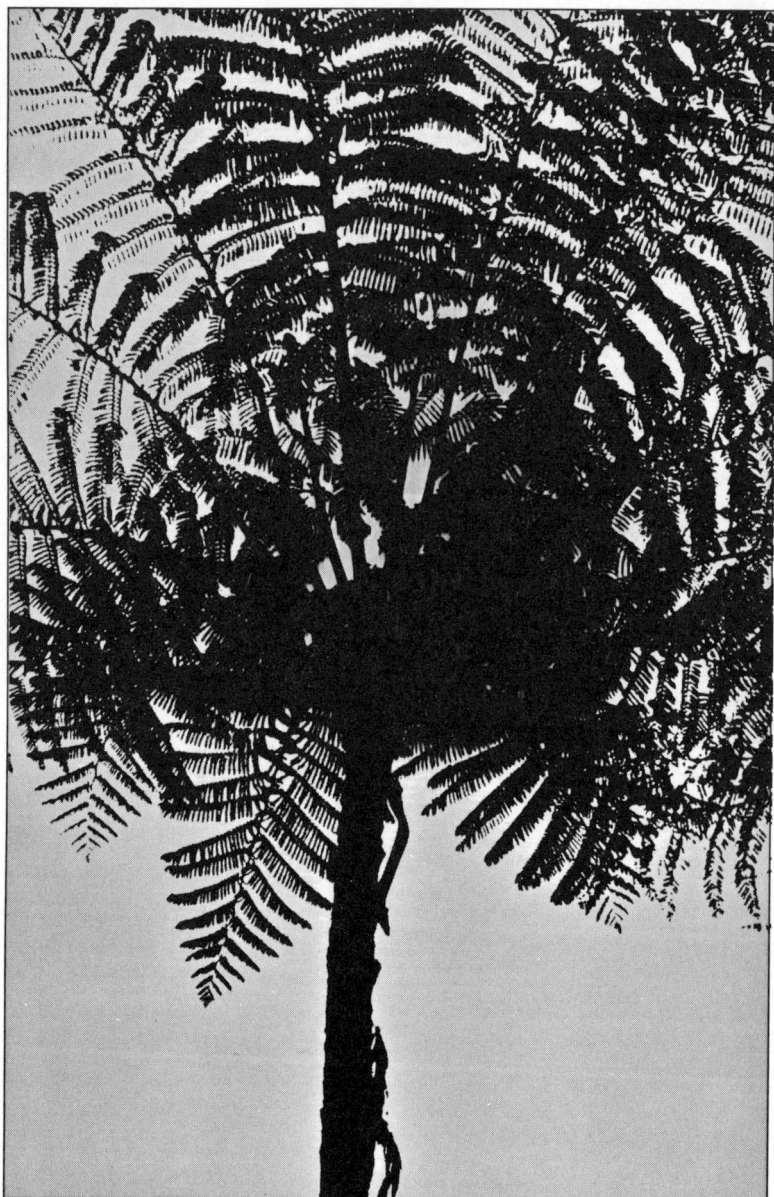